The HOPE of ELIZA

Tawnye Dee Kanumuri

Copyright © 2014 Tawnye Kanumuri.

All rights reserved. No part of this book may be used or reproduced by any means, graphic, electronic, or mechanical, including photocopying, recording, taping or by any information storage retrieval system without the written permission of the publisher except in the case of brief quotations embodied in critical articles and reviews.

WestBow Press books may be ordered through booksellers or by contacting:

WestBow Press
A Division of Thomas Nelson & Zondervan
1663 Liberty Drive
Bloomington, IN 47403
www.westbowpress.com
1 (866) 928-1240

Because of the dynamic nature of the Internet, any web addresses or links contained in this book may have changed since publication and may no longer be valid. The views expressed in this work are solely those of the author and do not necessarily reflect the views of the publisher, and the publisher hereby disclaims any responsibility for them.

Any people depicted in stock imagery provided by Thinkstock are models, and such images are being used for illustrative purposes only. Certain stock imagery © Thinkstock.

ISBN: 978-1-4908-3984-4 (sc)
ISBN: 978-1-4908-3986-8 (hc)
ISBN: 978-1-4908-3985-1 (e)

Library of Congress Control Number: 2014912252

Printed in the United States of America.

WestBow Press rev. date: 07/21/2014

Dear Reader,

    I am happy to present to you the Hope of Eliza. This book is a prime example of the unconditional love and relentless pursuit of our Savior. He alone has pursued us before we choose to follow him. The Bible says in Romans 5:8"But God demonstrates his own love for us in this: While we were still sinners, Christ died for us." He was willing to die for us in the hopes that we would choose to follow him. Even after we dedicate our life to Jesus we still fall. We still fail. Our story is about His righteousness rather than our ability to be righteous.

    Before we find God, we are lost and misguided. Many of our testimonies include mountains of costly mistakes before He found us. We are the redeemed because He chose us while we were still pursuing the pleasures of this world. That is the case for this book's main character Emma. Her struggles before she meets Jesus are many. Her life doesn't align with what God calls us to be. She is lost.

    For any first time readers let me caution you. This book deals with many sensitive issues and is not for young readers. It is recommended for a mature audience. Please screen for teen readers. The topics that are addressed in this book are sex outside of marriage, teenage pregnancy, abortion, suicide, drugs, alcohol, and child abuse.

    The Bible has things to say about all these issues. While all of these issues are addressed through a Biblical perspective with a positive message, this book is not appropriate for all audiences. Because it deals with such sensitive issues I have chosen to address these discreetly but honestly. It was a hard choice to make on exactly how much detail was required, but I hope that my readers understand why I chose to include what I did. The Bible does not skate around the truth of these issues, but openly proclaims what is good, noble, and pure.

    I hope this book challenges you, inspires you, and teaches you as you follow these women's fictional but realistic stories.

Tawnye Kanumuri

Acknowledgments

I would like to thank more than a few people for this book. Some people are unaware of how much truly goes into a novel.

A special thanks to my mom for encouraging me in my writing when I wrote my first book at age twelve. I would love to thank my dad for his passion about this book *The Hope of Eliza* and for his constant support of unborn children. To my husband who has been the wheels to my book. He has provided emotional support for my book, the finances to see it published, the time it took for me to write it, and endless conversations about the characters. He is also a supporting editor. I say he is the wheels to my book because he did so much research about publishing and helped me make my dreams of publishing come true. I would like to thank my siblings Nicki, Mandie- who was my test reader- Holly, Toby, Coby, Johnny, and Gracie who are very excited about the book. And a special thanks to my prayer warrior Nana.

I have to thank Jesus, without whom this book would never have been published. The prayers that have been directed to Him about this book could make a short story themselves. He has always listened to me, reassured me, and inspired me to write. This book comes from Him who birthed the story in me. Without His encouragement and support, I would have given up halfway through.

I would like to thank all the wonderful people I have worked with at WestBow Press who have encouraged me and answered my innumerable questions with upmost patience and knowledge. I am thankful to have found such a supportive team to make my dream a reality.

Thanks to Royal Family Kids Camp, Mercy Ministries, The Caring Pregnancy Center, The Tim Tebow Foundation, Eric Wilson and Theresa Preston, authors of *October Baby*, and to the creators of the movie, and many others who care for the moms' and unplanned babies' lives.

Prologue

As a smooth pebble dashes through the water, it makes ripples that start very large, but as they expand, they become calmer but wider and reach farther. So as people, our lives touch many others and we can't predict how much we're going to change the entire surface. Some pebbles make small changes, while others are boulder sized—each one touches every part of the still pond, affecting every reflection and causing energy to surge through the water.

Psychologists call this the ripple effect. The ripple effect is a beautiful picture of how one person's initial action (a pebble being tossed into the water) causes a reaction (the ripples) that touches more than one person and has an indirect effect on other people. For example, if you smile at one person, that would be the initial action. The direct impact is that that person feels important to you. The indirect effect (the ripple) might be that that person also smiles at another person whose day becomes better. This starts a chain reaction, where only the first action and the second are directly related, but all following actions are indirectly related.

In effect, we can't truly measure the impact that we have on other people in our lifetime. We can only assume that our direct impact may touch hundreds while our indirect actions may impact thousands. We don't know how far our ripple will carry, but we can be assured that mankind is connected in ways that we will never fully understand.

Chapter 1

Eliza smiled as only a little girl of three could smile. She had blonde hair like her mother and soft brown eyes like her father. She was wearing a pink dress picked out by Kathy, or as Eliza called her, Grammy. She ran up and down the small driveway leading into the apartment complex. She switched between chasing the boys who lived in the apartments next to them and riding her brand-new bike.

Her mother had only to look at her and a big proud smile would spread across her face. *Look at that little girl; she is so precious*, she thought. As much as she wanted her to stay little forever, she realized she was growing up. *I'm the luckiest mother in the world.*

"Mom." She bent over and sat next to Grammy on the steps. "Just look at how beautiful she is."

"She is definitely that," Grammy replied. "Not all girls are this blessed to have such a wonderful mother."

"I know." She smiled and winked at her unofficially adopted mom. Grammy only smiled and refocused her attention on the granddaughter who had captured her heart.

She stood, leaving the spot beside her mom, and went back into the house, knowing her daughter was safe with Grammy. She began to clean the apartment, which had become a disaster in just minutes. There was the wrapping paper on the floor that took all of five minutes to unwrap, dropped cake was smashed into the carpet, and the red juice had been spilled half a dozen times on the beautiful plastic tablecloth because Grammy had insisted on having matching paper cups, although most of the guests still sipped out of the nonspill kind. She smiled to herself and glanced out the window at her darling baby. Life was not always so perfect, but today was a special exception.

What would the future hold for this precious child? One could only imagine.

Fifteen years later

Eliza looked in the mirror again. This was her day to be dressed for success. She had finally graduated. High school had been fun but difficult, like all teen years. But at age eighteen, she wanted nothing more than a new direction, which she had found at the Simmons Publishing Corporation. The company had grown dynamically over the last nine years. It offered an internship for aspiring writers and publishers.

She was dressed for success, all right. Her elegant heels, black pinstriped pants, and matching top made her look quite professional despite her young age. She was ready for the interview, and she would do nearly anything to get this internship position. It only paid six hundred dollars a month in stipends, but it offered comfortable living accommodations at a complex that was on site and built just for the interns. She would have her own room on the top floor of the building, which was shared by the other interns. The money would provide enough for gas and expenses. Her mother helped her out by giving her the car, which was very generous considering her family's current state. Being a single parent had been hard on both mother and daughter. Still, Eliza couldn't complain. She and her mom were very close, and she wouldn't trade her mother for anything, not even for a two-parent home.

The company was located only six hours from home. *A quick little drive,* she thought. Plus she would be taking classes at the nearby university full time as part of the internship. That, however, had its own expense, and while it was not required to attend school, it was what she wanted to do. Besides, few interns had ever turned down the opportunity, considering the school offered a partial scholarship because of the internship. Plus the internship itself counted for multiple credits. Everything was working out wonderfully; glancing in the mirror, she found it to be true. Smiling, she headed out the door.

The world of opportunity awaited her.

Emma glanced at her tidy appearance. She was always perfect; however, today it was especially important to make sure she looked it. Emma was to receive a special award for her cheerleading abilities. She had choreographed their winning routine that earned them the state title. Of course, it was little surprise to Emma how well they had done. After all, she had scripted the routine herself. What started out as a class project for dance soon turned into a huge ensemble that had played over and over again in her mind. It included all the syllabus steps for cheerleading plus a little extra. With her strong dance background, which included everything from ballet to salsa, her vision for creating new moves was endless. Her coach had been surprised when Emma had approached her about an idea for the state routine. She suggested that Emma get some of her friends in on it to work up a mini routine that could be evaluated by herself and later by the entire cheerleading squad.

Emma didn't hesitate. She roped in some willing candidates, and before anyone knew it, they were all working on a slightly altered version of Emma's dance. She was unbelievably pleased with herself. While the coach always took suggestions, she never let anyone choreograph for competitions, but this routine had been just that good. Emma worked alongside the coach to ensure everyone performed their parts with precision. Oftentimes, she found herself staying late to do a private lesson with one of her teammates.

Well, their hard work had paid off. "We won state!" Her senior year couldn't have been more amazing if she had scripted it herself. This moment would stay with her forever. Now she was being honored at a special school event that recognized athletes. Of course, her super-hot boyfriend, Luke, had been awarded MVP on the football team and was now practicing with the basketball team. The banquet was thrown to honor the fall sports teams, which included cheer. She was so excited that she could hear her heart pounding. She imagined the moment in the dark auditorium at school. She would walk across the stage and accept the award with a proud smile. She couldn't wait to get to school.

Dad was going to be there. Normally far too busy with his million-dollar company, he had promised he'd be there. Emma didn't care to admit, even to herself, how much this truly meant to her.

"Can you believe I got the job?" Eliza squeezed her mom in a huge hug. She was practically jumping up and down.

"I'm so proud of you, sweetheart."

"I'm so happy. I mean, it was like they were actually impressed."

"Of course they were. You are very passionate about writing and about their program. I think they saw that."

"I know. I just can't believe this is happening."

"Let's call Grammy and tell her the good news. We should all go out and celebrate at Garden Gourmet."

"Mom, are you sure? That place is really expensive."

"Yes, but you've been dying to go there since it opened, and this is a special occasion. Besides, the outdoor-garden eating area rather intrigues me, and I've heard it's absolutely beautiful."

Eliza realized what a sacrifice her mom was making; however, she didn't want to make it worse by emphasizing that. Besides, she never won these debates. Her generous mother had always made sure her daughter never went without. Even on a one-parent income, that $250 prom dress, every birthday, every

Christmas, and any other dream Eliza had desired were all given with no hesitation. This day was no exception.

Someday, Emma wanted to be able to repay her mother. She wanted to spoil her. Her mom rarely spent on herself, only on Eliza. Grammy was so generous and often helped out as well. Emma wanted to spoil them in a few years. Massages, cruises—the possibilities were endless. This position would help secure her dream and all of their futures.

Emma was not disappointed. Thus far, her night had been perfect. Her dad had showed up looking dapper in his dark suit. He was still extremely handsome at age forty-three. He had light-brown, almost blond hair and a smile that could capture any woman's heart. Her mother, equally beautiful with long, blonde hair—so much like Emma's that they were often mistaken for sisters—was also there. Emma hoped she looked that good at forty. Her mother was skinny and wore a form-fitting knee-length black social dress. Her smile was also infectious. Together, they worked the room like the hosts at celebrity bashes.

Everybody had noticed their stunning appearance and that of their daughter. Emma looked amazing in the latest fashion-cut dress with a lovely, deep-burgundy color. The dress was very formal and fitted to every beautiful curve. It showed just a hint of cleavage. It was not immodest at all but just the right peek.

Luke blew her a kiss from across the stage. The award ceremony was like other award ceremonies—pretty boring until they called your name.

Afterward, Luke invited her to celebrate with the whole team. They decided to take his red sports car. Although older than Emma's car, its style was unquestionable. He told Tommy to ride in the back because "his girl" was going to sit next to him. Holding his hand in the fancy Camaro, she felt like Princess Jasmine on a magic carpet ride. She still held her stylish trophy with her name etched in gold letters. Could the night get any better?

Emma's dream night was slowly coming to a close. Luke had dropped Tommy off first in order to ensure they had some alone time and some privacy to say good night properly. Putting the car in park, Luke draped his arm around her and kissed the top of her head.

"I love you," he whispered, "and I'm proud of you."

Emma smiled to herself, taking in his alluring scent. Her right arm clung to his shirt, and her eyes danced with fire.

"I love you too, baby."

She smiled up at him and moved her arm slowly up his chest. He embraced her and kissed her as only he could. Pulling back a minute later, she smiled at him, breathless. His brown eyes danced with excitement. His blond hair, usually perfect, was out of place due to their amazing kiss.

"I don't want you to go." His incredible smile never ceased to throw Emma slightly off balance, as if she was teetering on the edge of a hill afraid but excited to ride down. Her eyes never left his face. "I could stay with you forever, but then my daddy would have to shoot you for keeping me out so late."

"Okay," he relented, but not before one more magical kiss that left both Emma and Luke hungering for more.

Emma got out of the car one high-heeled shoe at a time, gently closed the door, and said good night. He waved from the car window and Emma stood shivering on the porch till he was out of sight. *My, that boy is dreamy.*

Emma climbed the stairs ever so quietly and flung off her shoes, collapsing into bed. *Definitely a perfect night*, she thought.

Garden Gourmet had been every bit as exciting as everyone had been hyping it up to be. The mood was romantic, the food fantastic. Eliza might have paid just for the setting alone. She had lost herself, daydreaming about what it might be like to have her wedding here and about how much it would cost. *Way too high*, she thought, and then she ventured her absurd idea out loud. "Wouldn't this be a great place to have my wedding?"

"Absolutely," replied her mother, not ceasing to smile or even hesitating.

Eliza wondered how she did it at all. Her mother could always dream, always hope, no matter their present realities. She had never discouraged Eliza either. In fact, she was always the one pressing these dreams until they seemed just short of reality.

"Now who's getting married?" Grammy spoke in a honey-sweet voice. She winked at Eliza and laughed. "Who's the lucky guy?"

"Come on, Grammy. You know there is no one special yet."

"No," her grandmother feigned shock. "Well," she added more seriously, "perhaps you'll find him on this little adventure of yours."

"Who knows?" her mother added. "He might be a self-made millionaire."

"Oh, Mother."

"It could happen. My daddy is rich."

Eliza nearly stopped breathing. Her mother rarely spoke about her real parents that Eliza had never even met. She longed for her to elaborate. This seemed to be one of the first memories that had brought a smile to her mother's face rather than tears. Her mother had been wealthy?

All of a sudden, Eliza was unexplainably angry. Though it wasn't their responsibility, surely they could have pitched in a few times. Maybe helped with the education expenses at least. Eliza had always wondered what had happened to them. Her mother always spoke of them in the past tense. Because of this, and the fact that they had adopted Grammy, Eliza had always believed that they died an early death. The journalist in her wanted to find out. However, tonight, of all nights, Eliza couldn't ruin, no matter how important the topic was. Perhaps tonight was a night to be on top for once.

Everything was picture-perfect right now. Eliza could only hope that it would be the same in her future career as well. Perhaps this day would mark the beginning of them changing their fate in the world. Who knew? Maybe one day, when the right man came along, they could actually afford this place.

Smiling, she joined the buzzing conversation between her grandmother and mother, which her train of thoughts had caused her to miss out on. No, tonight was beyond perfect. Enough time for messes later.

Chapter 2

"Congratulations, Emma."

"Yeah, congrats." People Emma had never even talked to had congratulated her on her success. Emma smiled, genuinely happy that everyone was making such a fuss. She couldn't wait to see Luke. He always met her for lunch near their locker just after this next class. She longed for a little peck on the cheek or even a strong arm around her waist. Emma didn't think she was done celebrating. Tomorrow was Saturday, so she was thinking a romantic evening for the two of them might be in order.

Just then, Sara walked up, beaming. "So did you enjoy last night?"

"Of course, I did."

"How much?" her friend pleaded. "I need details."

"About what?"

"About you and Luke. Tommy said you guys dropped him off early."

"We did not! It was nearly eleven on a school night."

"But still, you must have celebrated somehow."

Emma got the remote feeling her friend was pushing for something specific. The confused look on her face must have showed, because Sara blurted out, "Well, did you do it or not?"

"Sara! I can't believe you. Luke and I don't have that kind of relationship."

"Why not? You're perfect for each other, right?"

"I'm not comfortable. We're both so young."

"Oh, Emma, you are so naïve. I bet you are the only virgin in the entire senior class."

"Not ahhh," Emma stated sharply. "And that's none of your business."

"Well, has he ever asked you?"

"Look, Luke is a gentleman, and the details of our personal lives are *personal*!"

"Okay. Touché. I didn't know until now that you were serious about this whole thing."

"You mean being a virgin. Well, it's not like there hasn't been opportunities."

"What's the problem then?"

"I don't know if it's right."

"You think it's wrong?"

"Yes, I mean … I don't know. I guess if it's the right person it's okay."

"You mean Luke's not the right one? Come on, you two have been dating for two years."

"I didn't say he wasn't the right person."

"Then what? I think you're just scared. I mean Luke's probably done it before …"

"Sara!" she said, embarrassed. "Just drop it, okay? You don't know what you're talking about."

"Okay, okay. Look, its fine. I don't think badly of you if you're not … You know. It's your business. I'm just curious. If he asked, would you say yes?"

Emma had never been more uncomfortable in all her life. Sure, she hadn't slept around, but that didn't make her undesirable like her friend was making her feel. And yes, Luke had never asked. Why should he? They were only in high school. Her friends always teased her about being innocent, but Emma suddenly began to wonder if they had ever actually believed that she was a virgin. After all, it wasn't as if she advertised it. Sure, she had dated before, and some of those guys had wanted more, but she wasn't stupid. No guy deserved her just because he dated her. But Luke … He was different; they were in love. She hoped they would get married. *Would she, if he asked?*

She had no answer to give Sara or herself. Her gut instinct said no, because it was wrong. Or was it? The only one who said it was wrong was God, and she didn't even believe in Him. Her parents weren't

Christians either. She doubted they would want her sleeping around, but they had never really even said as much. She sighed, wishing her burning cheeks would return to a normal color.

"Guess I won't tell," she responded with a smirk to cover up her churning emotions. "Come on. We'll be late for class."

Emma contemplated what Sara had said for all of about two minutes. Who cared what Sara thought anyway? Sara was known for her womanly ways and had a matching reputation. However, that never stopped her from snagging the hottest guys at school. Or maybe her reputation had helped her rather than hurt her in the dating department. Sara seemed to fit in socially, but Emma didn't consider them exceptionally close friends. Besides, Emma had no desire to win the kind of reputation Sara seemed to flaunt. It was enough for her that she had Luke. After all, not even Sara had snagged him. If he was happy and so was she, then she didn't care. And if Sara wanted to start rumors that she had never been with anyone, so what? No one would believe them anyway, even if it was true. Emma had worked to get to where she was. People trusted her to be the most up to date on relationships, styles, gossip, and anything else remotely important. So what if she was a virgin? No one would care. Besides, no one wanted to cross Luke; he could be extremely protective and was known not give a crap who you were socially. He'd stand up to anyone he thought was wrong, especially if they were hurting *his girl.*

Yep, nothing to worry about.

"Hey, girl."

"Hi, Jordyn."

"Hey, before the class starts, I wanted to ask you: want to go to the mall? They are having some big sale or something, and I could really use some time away from my house, if you know what I mean?"

"Yeah, I do," Emma said. But in truth, she had never *needed* to get out of the house. She almost never fought with her parents. They had always been close or at least close enough not to fight. Mom was picky about some things, like the condition of how she kept her room, but she wasn't controlling like Jordyn's mom. She had her moments but didn't put a lot of restrictions on what freedom Emma had. As long as she followed the rules of a clean house and good grades, nothing else seemed to matter to her mother. And as for Dad, she had never talked to him without him smiling at her. Though their talks were rare, he exploited every moment to catch up with his daughter and never seemed to be anything but pleased with her.

Of course, Emma wasn't hard to deal with either. She was pretty independent from an early age and very responsible. She was a rule follower and generally never tried to press those boundaries. Her family didn't have a lot of other issues either. Money had never been an issue or a stress. She didn't complain about Dad being gone, because the times she did see him were always so wonderful. Besides, her mom was always there, though mostly she had her own hobbies to worry about. Her home was comfortable with plenty of space and always had the best food.

Her best friend, Jordyn, on the other hand, had a wild side. Though Emma went to the outrageous parties, she never drank. She and Luke ignored the drugs and just had a good time. Jordyn always had to experience things. She would try anything and make up her own mind about it later. She wasn't perfect, and Emma guessed she would have pushed even a rational mom a little overboard. However, Jordyn's mom seemed a little on the crazy side. She was a control freak who needed to know every detail of each person in the household's lives. She ran the whole family. Emma thought that if she could take a chill pill, then Jordyn wouldn't feel the need to assert her opinion and independence. Likewise, if Jordyn was a tiny bit more responsible, perhaps her mother would loosen up, or maybe not. Maybe that was how Jordyn got to be the way she was in the first place. No one should control another person's life; it could only last so long.

"I'd love to. I want to see if those shoes are still there. I may just have to buy them."

"You should. They looked great on you. I'm sure Luke would love them."

At the mention of Luke's name, Emma glanced at the clock. "Forty-five minutes till lunch. You have got to be kidding me." Her friend just smiled knowingly and turned her attention back to the teacher.

Packing up the Honda had been more difficult than Eliza had imagined. Her mom was running around like her head was going to fall off. Every few minutes, she would say, "Don't forget this," and hold up an old photo of them together, or Eliza's favorite stuffed animal or an old couch blanket.

"Mom, I'm fine. It's not like I'll never be home again. I can only pack the essentials. It's not like I'm buying a house."

"I know, dear. I just don't want you to forget anything important." She sighed. "Well, I guess you should head out so you can make it before dark. Do you have the emergency credit card in case something goes wrong? Did I give you enough gas money?"

"Yes, it's in my purse."

"Double-check, sweetheart."

"Mom …"

"Just one last time. I need to know you have it." Sighing, Eliza headed out to the car to retrieve her purse. She might never get a chance to leave.

"Darling, you have to let her go. Come on. Let's meet her at the car," Grammy said quietly from the couch she had long since resigned herself to. She had come over nearly two hours ago to say good-bye. So much for that.

"I know it's just that this house already seems empty without her. For eighteen years, she's all I've had to love." She swiped a tear. "Okay, here we go." Squaring her shoulders and straitening her shirt, she met her daughter on the curb.

"Bye, Eliza."

Eliza glanced back to see her mother trying to hold herself together. Grammy stood next to her, offering her arm as support—emotional support.

All of a sudden, it seemed harder for Eliza too. She felt like she couldn't leave her mom all alone in this two-bedroom townhouse, with no one to talk to or to listen to how her day went. Dozens of food-shopping trips flashed through her mind and images of little coffeehouses that they had chatted in suddenly appeared. Yet if someone didn't make a move, no one would be able to hold it together much longer. Plus Eliza knew Grammy would take over. She loved them both so much. She was nothing short of a godsend. Eliza truly believed that she had come around at the right time for her mother.

She trudged over to them to say good-bye. "Oh, Mom, I'm going to miss you. I'll miss you both. Thanks so much for everything." She swallowed them both in a large bear hug.

"Love you too, sweetheart."

"Have a safe journey, Eliza," Grammy said. And then she prayed that Eliza would indeed have a pleasant journey.

Eliza stepped out of the group hug they had formed and smiled. "Bye," she whispered, barely audibly.

Then she drove away, Grammy and Mom waving until she was out of sight.

At first, the open road had provided some privacy to grieve over their good-byes, and then it offered freedom and hope, and now the closer she got, it offered sleep. Sleep sounded really good after an emotionally draining day.

Eliza finally arrived. She parked the car, grabbed one overnight bag, and left the rest for in the morning. Now she needed sleep. She signed in and then was given keys to her room. She shoved the big door open to reveal a rather large, almost hotel-looking room.

It had a queen-size bed with an attached bath, a regular-size closet, and opposite to the bed was a desk with its own lamp. The only thing that set it apart from a hotel room was the lack of maids and a large built-in bookshelf right next to the computer desk. Thoughtful, considering college students had a few too many books to store. The room also held a tiny counter with a small refrigerator and a microwave, which was located to the right side of the bed, and of course, the essentails a dresser unit with a flat-screen TV on top. Two darling little nightstands stood on each side of the bed. *Who is the second one for?* Eliza laughed to herself. Perhaps its purpose was mostly aesthetic.

She kicked off her shoes, set her alarm, and plugged in her phone. She texted her mother, who had been waiting up to make sure she made it all right, and then slipped between the soft covers.

Yeah, she could get used to this space of her own.

"Emma!"

"Yeah, Mom," she called down.

"Luke is here to pick you up."

"One minute." Emma finished brushing her hair. She double-checked the ever-lying mirror to make sure everything was perfect and then hurried downstairs to catch up with Luke. "Hey, baby," she said, kissing his cheek.

"Are you ready?" Luke asked.

"Yep. I just need to grab my jacket."

"Where are you guys going?" Mom asked casually.

"To the park."

"Okay, well, what time will you be getting home?"

"In an hour or so, right, Luke?"

"Yeah, whenever. Do you need her home by a certain time, Mrs. Steward?"

"No, but I have to do some errands. I wanted to be home in time to finish our game of dominos, if you two don't have anything better to do."

Emma smiled. Her mom was usually extremely busy being a homemaker. She tended to spend at least an hour preparing each meal. Plus she maintained their home as if it were a model home—not a speck of dust in any corner. Today she was the one who suggested they hang out. Dominos was the one game where Mom let her guard down. She laughed and joked right alongside her and Luke. Dominos was a fun family game. Occasionally, even Dad joined.

"Sure thing, Mom." Emma planted a kiss on her mother's cheek and followed Luke out the door.

"It's a really nice day to go to the park," Luke explained. "I brought the Frisbee too."

Emma smiled. There weren't very many days Luke didn't have some kind of sports equipment or game in mind. He usually was extremely competitive, but not when he played with Emma. No matter if Emma was good or not, he made whatever game they played enjoyable. Seizing her chance for a bit of fun, Emma took off running. Normally, it was just a short walk to the park.

"Hey, Emma, wait up." Her ploy was working. Luke was chasing her. Maybe he might have a chance at catching up.

Luke could play this game too. Instead of throwing himself into a full run, he jogged a little behind her. Emma let out an endearing little shrill as he pursued her. Then, just before she was about to let off since they had reached the park, Luke pushed off the ground and ran at her as hard as he could.

Emma turned back just in time to see him close the distance. Luke knocked her off her feet and held her head so it didn't land smack onto the hard ground. Much to Emma's surprise, that was not enough; he had more planned.

After they both toppled over, Luke immediately started tickling her. This was Emma's weakness. "Stop ... Luke," she managed. "Please. Okay ... That's it! ... No more kisses today for you," she taunted, a little out of breath. Luke just smiled and continued tickling her until she got mad. She began pounding him playfully and screamed, "I mean it, Luke Howard! Stop it!" Luke let her shove him to his feet. In mock rage, Emma scolded, "Luke, you meanie! I should just go home right now."

"Oh, I'm sorry, sweetheart," he soothed in a playful tone. "Are you out of air?"

That was the last draw for Emma. She walked straight up to him, knocked his baseball cap to the ground, and stomped away.

Luke smiled. *Boy, she was cute when she got angry.* "Emma, let me make it up to you. I'm sorry." This time, the words were half-sincere. He whirled her around and pulled her into his arms. Emma pretended to be angry, burying her face in his chest. Though he couldn't see, she was smiling from head to toe.

"Hey, Mom, we're back."

"Okay, sweetheart, let me just put these brownies in the oven."

"Are they for us?"

"Yeah. I thought we might eat a few while we played."

"Yum, thanks, Mom."

"Yeah, thanks, Mrs. Steward."

"Luke, get out the dominos, will you? I'll be over just one sec."

The Hope of Eliza

Emma glanced at Luke, who was already carrying out her instructions.

"Okay, where were we? Oh yeah ..." Her mother smiled teasingly. "I was kicking your butts."

"Not uh," Emma retorted. "I'm right behind you."

The three played the rest of the game with many laughs and jokes. Mom won again, with Emma coming in second and Luke far behind like usual. When he got up to leave, Emma walked him out.

"Luke, honey, you're not staying for dinner?" her mother said in surprise.

"No, Mrs. Steward, unfortunately not. It appears my mom actually misses me sometimes," he joked. "She made me promise I'd be home by six."

"She's making his favorite: meatballs," Emma filled in.

"Oh, shame. That's what we are having," her mother teased. "Bye, Luke."

"Bye, Mrs. Steward. Bye, baby. See you tomorrow."

"I know. It's Friday, the weekend at last. Do you want to go out Saturday?"

"Yeah, sure, let's make plans tomorrow. I really gotta go."

"Okay, bye." He kissed her and then walked down the steps. Thank goodness, it was Friday; Emma was already tired of school. Senioritis. Yeah, she had it bad.

Chapter 3

The fifteen interns entered the auditorium room, which was quite large and looked like it was used primarily for guest speakers. There was a small stage in the front that was only about two feet high. In front of the stage were close to five hundred office-looking chairs with an aisle between them. At the very back of the auditorium, opposite the stage, the whole wall was filled with floor-length windows. The windows reached up at least fifteen feet. All of them were rectangular and let in a ton of natural light. The drapes were simple and left open for the time being. Other than that, the large room was rather empty. The two long walls on either side of the stage each held a single picture frame. On the right, facing the stage, was a huge map of the world. The quote read, "To be successful, one must learn that the world is a rather large place and that you are merely one person in it."

Eliza thought it might have been referring to both vision and humility. The wall opposite held only a small frame that she couldn't read and a few tiny plaques that held awards the company must have earned. To the right of the plaques were pictures of the major people in the company, with their names written underneath.

Eliza turned her attention to Mr. Grant, who was introducing himself. He looked to be in his early forties with brown hair with a hint of red in it. He had glasses on and brown, expensive leather shoes. He was wearing khaki pants and a blue blazer with a white shirt underneath. Though he was not very interesting to look at, his smile was attractive, and his voice carried a lot of authority. Furthermore, his voice had a rhythm that was easy to listen to.

"I am the director of public relations for this company, and I also oversee our interns, so perhaps I should have introduced myself as your boss."

A quiet chuckle followed his statement. Although there was nothing extremely humorous about the statement, it was how he said it that brought a smile from the audience.

"I'm sure you all have a million questions, which I will take after the tour. However, before that, I'm afraid I have some bad news." Mr. Grant continued. "Even though you have been accepted into this program, there are only enough for five of you to get scholarships at the school. You all will still earn the college credit, but you won't all get the scholarship. Now I called the financial aid department and told them I had fifteen interns, and they were all expecting scholarships. They said there wasn't enough funding this year because of budget cuts. They went back and forth with me and finally said they would give us eight to work with and that I would have to choose who received them.

"So since there is about two months until the school semester starts, that is my deadline. That gives you two months to prove to me that you will be a valuable asset to this company. However, I know some of you can't afford to stay here without it, so I will take financial situations into account the best I can. However, your best chance at receiving one will be proving that you belong here. Please, jot down your financial needs on the note cards that are being passed around. Kindly hand them to me after the meeting is over. There is no need to try to convince me to award you a scholarship. I will decide primarily based on your skills and work ethic. Sorry about that bit of bad news."

He quickly moved on to other topics. Clearly, he wasn't that stressed about the scholarship money. After all, he was a businessman and needed to get back to business. Eliza thought of her mother. Already she had sacrificed so much to send her here. Without the scholarship, would she be able to stay? After all, she was already taking out student loans for the part of her education that the scholarship didn't help out with. Her mother was scraping every penny together for the rest of the tuition that the loans didn't cover. Her only thought now was that she had to be a scholarship winner to get the money. She glanced around at all the suddenly serious faces.

There was a beautiful blonde with long hair. It was curled slightly at the ends and pulled back into an elegant ponytail. She was wearing a fashionable tan skirt with a calico-brown pattern and a yellow, short-sleeve collared top. Eliza thought she had introduced herself as Annie. She seemed like a very nice girl, but judging by her dress and how she presented herself, she was a hard-to-beat professional.

Even now while Eliza's mind wandered, she sat there patiently, listening with a look on her face that said she was interested in what Mr. Grant had to say and that she completely understood all of it. Then there was Josh. Judging only from first impressions, Eliza would say he lived a carefree life off Daddy's money and could be quiet charming with the ladies, which usually meant he could also be a spoiled jerk.

His dark hair and slightly tan complexion made him immediately attractive. However, he came off … How could she put it? Kind of fake, like plastic.

Maybe she was judging him too harshly. He had been nice enough to her, although their introduction was a matter of mere seconds while waiting for the orientation to begin. She knew nothing about the brunette sitting next to him. She had exceptional long hair and a lonely look on her face. While everyone else had been chatting beforehand, she had been silently observing without saying a word. She was dressed nice enough but gave off a tomboy look. Then there was the redhead, who never stopped talking, that was sitting next to her. She had animated facial expressions and looked like the cheerful morning type. The last person she recognized was a tall man with jet-black hair and an easy smile. He was a little older, probably close to his thirties. No doubt he was already well educated, but he was probably hoping to snag a job here by the end of the internship. Another lady, with light-brown hair, was sitting next to him. She also seemed to be a bit older than Eliza. However, she had snuck in just as the meeting began so no one had had a chance to talk with her. She contemplated the man sitting in front of her. He kind of looked like a younger and geekier version of Mr. Grant. His name was … Oh yeah. John. The others she hadn't gotten a chance to talk to yet, but with only fifteen interns, she would know them all soon.

That night, Eliza dialed up her mom to let her know how the first day had gone. "It was wonderful. Mr. Grant seems nice, even kind of funny. He also, seems really knowledgeable. I think I am going to learn a lot. He took us all out to lunch this afternoon—the company's treat. He has some fascinating success stories. I can't wait till this weekend is over so I can get started."

Her mother seemed pleased to hear all of this. "That's wonderful, honey. I'm so glad you like it, but I already miss you."

"Me too, Mom. There is one small piece of bad news." She relayed what Mr. Grant had said about the scholarship and then added, "But don't worry, I'm sure I will get one of those spots. I'll make you proud."

"I'm sure you will, sweetheart. Don't worry. Just do your best."

"I will. Talk to you tomorrow, Mom. Love you."

"Love you too, Lizzy."

Mom was the only one she let call her Lizzy. She much preferred *Liza*. *Lizzy* didn't make much sense since the *i* no longer said its long vowel sound as in *Eliza*. However, most of the time, Mom called her Eliza—never Liza and only sometimes Lizzy. Well, she was her mother's daughter, after all. No one could deny her the parental right of an affectionate nickname. She smiled and then turned to her laptop. She had a journal article she had been dying to publish. Maybe this was her chance.

Luke picked her up looking as handsome as ever. He drove her downtown for a surprise. Emma wasn't up for many surprises. Though she trusted Luke, she always had a need to know what was going on. He enjoyed seeing her antsy though. Luke was the kind that believed surprises were romantic.

"Okay, Luke, where are we going?"

"None of your business."

"It is too, Luke. This is my date night too."

Luke looked to his right, at her small, pouty face. He laughed a little, but not out loud. That would only fuel her fire. It was going to be a good surprise. It was only eight o'clock, but the sky had already begun to darken. The lights from downtown created a festive and romantic atmosphere. Luke knew surprises didn't have to get complicated or expensive. He was taking her somewhere she had always talked about going but never gone: Henry's.

Henry's was an old-fashioned ice-cream soda shop. It had a wooden porch and barstools at the main counter. The place was always a little on the chilly side, so he had even thought of that. He brought along his high school jacket for Emma to wear. She looked so cute in her skirt and blouse and thin sweater, but she'd be freezing in five seconds.

As he came closer, he told her to close her eyes. Reluctantly, she did. He pulled the Camaro smoothly into the last parking space. It happened to be right in front of the shop. *Wow, on a Saturday night downtown. Lucky me.* He opened her door and helped her down so she didn't kill herself because she was still closing her eyes. He turned her gently toward Henry's, his fingers resting lightly on her shoulders. Henry's was fashioned with the décor of a typical drugstore in the 1950s. The barstool and soda fountain looked authentic. The wooden floors looked aged too. Even, the front porch and the sign looked like they were from the 1950s.

"Okay, open."

A slight gasp escaped her mouth, and her small arms flew around his neck. "You're the best boyfriend in this whole town, Luke Howard."

A smile that matched Emma's was spread across his face. He loved making her happy. Taking her by the hand, he led her to the barstool. After she sat, he gently laid the jacket over her slender shoulders. She flashed him a grateful and impressed smile. Then she spent the next fifteen minutes trying to decide what she wanted and finally narrowed it down to two options.

When the waiter came by, he glanced at them. "Are you guys ready?" he asked cautiously. He had already been denied the two previous times he had asked.

Before she could respond, Luke said, "Yes, sir, we need two root beer floats and one peanut butter cherry sundae." Emma started to object, telling Luke she only needed one, but he sent her a be-quiet look, and she just giggled. Luke spared no expense to make her happy. A quality she loved about him.

"You are wonderful, love. I've always wanted to go here."

"I know. That's why I brought you here."

"Yes, but I'm surprised you remembered."

"What's important to you is etched in my mind forever, because you're my girl." She smiled and let her mind drift. It felt so good to be loved. She couldn't help but love him back.

Chapter 4

Eliza crossed the parking lot to the interns' office on the fifth floor, which resembled a nice computer lab in high school. There were desks, real ones, pushed together instead of tables. There weren't even cubicles to separate them from one another. The interns worked in the open in one room, some side by side and others separated only by their computer monitors. However, each one had a comfy burgundy office chair and a spacious desk that contained file cabinet drawers. In addition, they had the best computer equipment, including two large printers in the corner. There were white kitchen cabinets on the wall closest to the door, where everyone had congregated. The interns had been welcomed by fresh office coffee and those really large, moist muffins, as well as some orange juice. Eliza felt slightly awkward, as did the others, judging by how no one had taken their seats.

Just then, Mr. Grant walked in. "Welcome, everyone. Feel free to take a seat wherever you like. This isn't high school; we don't have assigned seating." Everyone let out a nervous chuckle, but no one moved.

Everyone seemed to delay, rather awkwardly, until the two oldest of the group—Jim and Stephanie—took their seats. Naturally, they would sit together, probably feeling more comfortable sitting next to each other rather than by all the young people. Eliza noticed they claimed the seats facing the door and the white board, toward the front of the room. Josh took a seat next to Annie on the very front row. He wouldn't last there very long, judging from the slight scowl that had crossed Annie's exquisite features. Apparently, there wasn't any room in her life for immature boys, no matter how good-looking. He tried to start up a light conversation while Annie glanced nervously around the room as if she had made a bad seating choice. Perhaps she was trying to conjure a polite way of excusing herself from her chosen seat. However, the seats were filling up now as all of the interns were heading for the desks. Eliza's hesitation made her choice for her, and she moved toward the corner, where two empty desks stood side by side along the same wall as the kitchen cupboards. It was also near the door to the conference room, which was on the opposite wall from the front door.

Eliza sighed. "I guess I'll be sitting alone. Oh well. Perhaps I'll get more work done over here." Or was she just saying that to make herself feel better? Even Kent, who seemed a little unsocial, found a seating partner between John (Mr. Grant Jr.) and Danny. Danny seemed cool. He had the look of a nice guy. He seemed easygoing and friendly with everyone. Why hadn't she sat near him?

Before she could finish her thought, Mr. Grant started the day by introducing a girl Eliza hadn't even noticed had been standing beside him. *Had she just come in?*

"And we have one latecomer. Everyone, welcome Kate."

The shy girl glanced at the floor before smiling at those seated in front of her. She cautiously scanned the room, not resting on any one person for more than a second. That is, until her eyes found Josh. Her jaw dropped slightly and a look of pure panic crossed her face before she could recompose herself. Josh merely smiled a little evil smirk and pushed back in his chair. Eliza wished the other two legs of the chair would lose footing and send him crashing to the floor. Something about that smirk made her want to punch him. Kate finally found the one open desk in the corner next to Eliza. She smiled slightly, nodding to Eliza, her new companion, and took her seat. As soon as she sat, Mr. Grant started in right away. He explained what their daily routine would look like, when they were expected to be in the office, and when they could work away from their desks. He encouraged people not to try working in the dorms, as it was often unproductive, but said it was completely up to them.

"You will be editing, filing, reading, evaluating, and hopefully publishing some pieces yourself. Above all, you must seek out opportunities to apply your skill wherever you can in this company. You can obviously guess why this would be advantageous."

"Emma, listen to this new song." Luke's charming smile lit up the whole hallway but was only directed at Emma. Luke was crazy about every kind of music. He always carried around his very expensive iPod and headphones, even at school. Emma glanced at the headphones, not knowing what was in store.

"That song reminds me of us," he said seriously.

"Oh, really?" she cooed. "Let me hear." She reached for the headphones.

Luke moved closer so that the headphones could reach. He kissed her cheek and placed the headphones around her ears. Immediately, she was transported to a new world. The music floated harmoniously, mixed with the lyrics of "You and I were made for each other ... breathing in the same air ... caught up in the same dream."

"That's beautiful," she whispered. "You really nailed that one." Luke smiled. *Wow! Can he make my heart melt!*

He felt the same way watching how she let the music carry her to some other place. Man, did he love this girl.

The next several weeks flew by for Eliza. She had gotten to know most of the interns, especially Kate, whom she sat next to. Kate was quiet at first but was opening up to Eliza slowly. Eliza was patient because the more she found out about Kate, the more she could see them becoming great friends. Kate had a unique perspective on life. The way she used everyday language and put it into poetry boggled Liza's mind. She had the finesse of a fine seamstress and so much patience with others and her work. She wasn't from a well-off family and, like Eliza, hoped to earn one of the scholarships.

Surprisingly, the office had changed dramatically from that first day. For one thing, an intern had already decided this fast-paced lifestyle was not for him. Mr. Grant had high expectations and fast deadlines. Within a week, he was gone. Another thing that had evolved was the relationships among the interns. Most everyone was very friendly and the group was becoming quite close, considering everything they were going through together. Different people were starting to hang out, and sometimes they'd all do something together. Stephanie and Jim were casually dating now.

Each intern was being trained for a specific purpose. A lot of their research and seminars focused on what was changing in journalism and publishing. Some were specifically researching new authors, others newspapers and journals, but all of the seminars focused on changing technology and social media, including Facebook and blogs. They also had individual jobs within the company. Some interns researched for current authors and were used as references for their next big book. Others helped find new talent and ideas. These people were required to propose ideas to the company's bigwigs. *Scary.*

Still others were starting to dive into the world of editing, which unfortunately was a vast world that required many of the interns' talents. Every few weeks, the interns were also given assignments to write their own pieces. Sometimes, these were published in the company's own magazine, in the local newspaper, or online! Eliza and Kate were two of the many on the editing team. Josh, with his charisma, was a natural choice to send to the board, although someone had to keep his feet on the ground. So naturally, and unfortunately for her, Annie was that person.

Although the two of them had to spend endless hours together, they were still not getting along. The balance brought into the team was Tina, who looked like she stepped out of a magazine every morning. Josh's attention quickly switched directions, which seemed to satisfy not only Annie but Tina and Josh as well. She had dark skin and dark hair and was pretty tall. She was Miss Fashionista—always looked good—and she knew how to do her makeup like she was a runway model.

"The love triangle is at it again." Kate rolled her eyes.

Eliza smiled and tried to ignore it, but by now, the conversation had elevated so that everyone in the room could hear. Eliza sighed but quickly found a way to distract herself. "You never told me why you hate him so much."

"What do you mean I hate him?"

"Josh. I mean, come on. We all remember the look on your face when you first saw him; you must have known him before."

"I don't want to talk about it." Eliza would have pushed her a little, had it not been for Annie leaping angrily from her seat.

Without realizing she had an audience, the usually composed Annie shouted, "You just agree with him because you too are sleeping together!"

The dark expression that passed on Tina's face looked as if she might take a swing at Annie, but instead, she leaned into Annie and replied, "So what if we are? Are you jealous, Miss Perfect?"

"That's it. I can't take it anymore. I want out of this team. I would much prefer editing than you two." With that, Annie stormed out.

Suddenly realizing they were the center of attention, Josh asked, "Wanna join me for a small break?" Tina smiled and walked out the door without a word, never acknowledging the people who were staring at them.

"Wow. The prize students may not be lined up for the scholarships after all," replied Kent. Apparently, he was still holding a grudge that he had not been put on the ideas team in the first place. Eliza felt sorry for him. Although he was brilliant, he wasn't great with people. Obviously, Kent would disagree with that statement, but it was true.

Everyone seemed to return to their work, but some still whispered. "Are they really sleeping together?" "No one denied it." "Annie would be the one to know." "That's unprofessional." "Is that even allowed, since we're interns?"

The couple didn't return, but Annie came back shortly in high spirits. She was to move her desk next to John's and would begin working with the writers after some more training. "They'll get scholarships for sure," whispered Kate.

"But so will we," Eliza said as she winked. The two friends smiled. Eliza prayed that what she had said was true.

Emma sat daydreaming on her bed. Life was pretty ordinary and kind of perfect for her. She had her future plans worked out. She knew that she wanted to become a pediatrician. Her parents could afford to send her to any school in the country, or out of it, for that matter. She relished her social life. A spotlight seemed to follow her around when she was at school, as if she were an actor on the stage all the time.

In fact, secretly that was how she felt. On the outside looking in, nothing could be better, but that was only one side of her. There was a quiet void on the inside, which somehow made her feel as if what she was doing wasn't providing any meaning in her life. She felt disconnected, even from herself. Everything in her life seemed like she was living from the outside, not from her heart. The only thing that felt close to actually living was Luke. Her passion for him blew her away. He had only to come near, and desire would rise up inside her. Desire and passion are powerful elements that drive the soul.

Emma had never paid that much attention to the inside of her life. She was more concerned with circumstance: new clothes, new shoes, the latest gossip, the relationship drama, the school dances, the next football game, the next big party, the latest fashion. All these things swirled around inside her, never being let out and never resting. They kept her mind busy and her body active, but still there were these quiet moments where Emma was afraid to hear her own thoughts. Because if she did, she usually heard, *What are you living for? What is the purpose of your life? Come away and be peaceful and loved.* That last comment confused her the most. She was peaceful, not fighting with anyone. What exactly did *Come away* mean? Come where and with whom? The voice echoed in her head and the closest she ever got to quieting it would be to imagine herself on a beach, not thinking or feeling anything. Oh, in that dream, there was plenty of freedom.

The closest she ever felt to being alive was when she was with Luke. With him, she had a purpose and a dream. She lived for him—to be with him. She felt loved, and truly loved someone else. It was these moments that her heart, her inside world opened up. She came alive. Only, did Luke feel the same way? They had never talked about forever. Emma had given her whole heart to him with no thought of its safety. She didn't want to push him. He had to be the one to share his dreams with her. Luke loved her now, but did he want to love her like this forever? She was both uncertain and confident that he would. Until he shared his feelings with her, she would have to wait. She wasn't going to attach herself to him. It was their choice, so Luke had to make his part of that choice. In the meantime, Emma didn't worry too often. They were in love, faithful to each other, and utterly happy.

Chapter 5

"Hey, Kate, want to head over to the dorms? We could chat it up in my room."

"We should be working on our projects."

"And we have been, but I need a break. I'm about to go crazy."

"Yes, but this is the last assignment before he chooses the scholarship."

"Yes, but ..." Liza said, mimicking Kate's voice, "my brain can't think when I'm hungry. I bought some brownies to share."

"Okay, fine. A five-minute break won't hurt." Kate smiled and followed her friend out of the office.

Upon arrival, both girls flung themselves down on Eliza's comfy bed.

"See? Soooo much better already," she said.

"You're impossible."

"Already knew that. You sometimes sound like a familiar voice from my childhood. Namely, my mother," Eliza teased.

"Whatever. We're all adults now. Do what you like. Eat brownies all day." Eliza laughed. Even though Eliza herself was a hard worker, she was nothing compared to Kate. Kate needed Eliza and Eliza felt she needed Kate too.

The girls chatted happily about this and that. Eventually, the conversation moved into the direction of relationships. Somehow, Josh got brought up.

"I know you want to know the story, but it's humiliating."

"Really?" Then jokingly to lighten the mood, she said, "Then you have to tell me."

Kate paused and for a moment. Eliza didn't think she would share after all. Eliza waited patiently, not pushing her friend.

Finally, Kate spoke. "Josh was my best friend all through grade school. Then we became serious in high school. I thought he was the one for me. We dated freshman year. He started changing, becoming more popular, but he never excluded me. We dated for three years, and then junior year, I hear a rumor that he was with Leslie. Leslie was popular, pretty, on the girls' volleyball team. Not to reinforce stereotypes, but she was blonde and cute.

Of course, I didn't believe the rumors I heard. I had known Josh my whole life. He was the only normal thing about my life. We still had fun together and talked about being together forever. I confronted him about the rumor, but he denied it. Then three months later, he told me the whole truth that he and Leslie had been dating ever since the rumor started, that it just kinda happened. Apparently, I was the laughingstock of the whole school because he had been dating us both for three months, and I had no clue. No one even cared that Leslie had known the entire time and dated him anyway.

"I guess I just remembered a different Josh and still chose to date him even though I knew things weren't right between us. But sadly, I never dreamed he was cheating on me. We broke up, of course. It was nasty. I was humiliated, and he wasn't even sorry. He said things like, 'You are really naïve to think this would last forever. I mean, come on. We were just kids.' Et cetera. He never apologized, and when I said I didn't want to be friends, he said, 'Fine,' and that was the end of it. After Leslie, who only lasted four months, there was Jessie, Tanya, Sammy, and others I didn't bother to keep track of. I mean it's horrible enough to be cheated on, lied to, and humiliated, but it was worse losing my best friend. I guess I probably lost him a long time ago but just hadn't admitted it to myself.

"He turned mean, scowled at me in the halls, made sure I was labeled undateable, but he still isn't happy. He changes women like some people change clothes. I'm not exaggerating either. You watch. He hasn't changed. Annie: flop. Tina: now. And someone else: later."

"Don't you feel like warning them?"

"No, not really. You should know who a man is before you date him. Don't get me wrong. I feel sorry for his girlfriends, but at the end of the day, no matter what he did to other girls, they still dated him, still fell for him, and still got their hearts broken. I think it's pride, because they think it'll be different because they are the one for him, or something like that."

"I'm sorry."

"I'm sorry he's here. I thought I was going to escape his games."

"Wow, he seems like a real jerk."

"Yeah, and he just got here. Wait. It will get worse."

"Anything I can do?"

"Take my advice and fend off his passes."

"What? Like he'd be interested in me!"

"Oh, come on. You are super hot."

"Stop it."

"Stop being modest. Don't try to tell me guys aren't interested. I mean, you're blonde, sweet, thin, and have beautiful brown eyes."

"To be honest, I don't know why, but guys don't fall for me."

"Get out."

"No, I'm serious. Maybe it's because I have a reputation."

"What reputation?"

"You know: too serious, only looking for the love of her life, not a good time. I won't … you know … have sex before marriage."

"You act like it's a bad thing."

"No. I just know it's not a popular decision, especially in high school. It seems our generation feels that if you're in love it's fine, but it's not. That's what happened to my mom. They were so in love till he left her. I guess that's why my mom raised me to think of it differently. I'm waiting for the right guy. It makes it easier having less options because a lot of them aren't willing to wait. I'm not anybody's girl without a commitment. I think every woman deserves that."

"Yeah, but not many of us get it."

"Yeah. That is true for my mom. I remember playing on the swing while my mother sat on a park bench watching me when I was little. I was giggling. My mom looked up at me and then past me. Her expression changed from one of joy and amusement to one of deep sadness. Sometimes, my mother had these moments. They were rare but intense. I looked behind me to see what had made her so upset. There was a mom with a little girl about my age, and her dad walked in-between them holding both their hands. I watched as the dad stooped and whispered something into the little girl's ear that made her giggle. Then he turned to the mom. My heart broke too. I was envious of that little girl, though at the time, I didn't know why or what envy even was. I longed to be lucky enough to have a dad. My mom had always been enough for me up until that point. It was my earliest moment where I felt the loss of not having a father.

"My mom and I left soon after. On the way home, my mom kept wiping her eyes. Finally, once at home, she collapsed onto her bed in a fit of tears that soon turned into sobs. I didn't know what to do. I sat on the couch and cried too. I've always thought she deserved someone who was committed and would never leave. But I guess you are right. She never got it."

Kate stared intensely at her friend. "How old were you?"

"I think I was about six."

"That must be a painful memory for you to have remembered it from such an early age." Kate seemed lost in a memory of her own but then refocused her attention back to Eliza. "How did you get through it?"

"My mom and Grammy helped me through the rough moments." Kate felt a little envy at that. At least Eliza knew how it felt to have someone to care about you. What would she say if she knew about Kate's past and the fact that no one had been there to help her? In fact, the people who were supposed to help were the problem. It had always been that way for Kate until now. Kate was beginning to trust Eliza. She had this feeling that no matter what happened, Eliza would be the one to be there for her from this moment on, but after so much abuse of trust, Kate held back from opening up. She just wasn't ready to share it all.

"Are you ready to tackle that paper now?" Eliza asked.

"Sadly, yes. I have a good idea on what to write about."

"Great. Let's get started."

"Happy birthday, Emma, love! Honey, I'm so sorry your father just couldn't make it." Her mom gave Emma a quick hug and nonchalantly went back to baking as if it didn't matter. But it did matter to Emma.

"What? He didn't even call?"

"Don't act like that, Emma." Her mother rolled her eyes. "Of course, he tried to be here, but Bangkok

The Hope of Eliza

is rather far away, and he got delayed with some important people."

Of course, my mother can act coolly, Emma thought. *She's used to it. It has been that way ever since they got married.* Emma, however, was more sensitive. Did he think she didn't need him here on her eighteenth birthday?

Luke gave her a very sympathetic look that also pleaded with her not to push her mother and spoil the already dampened mood. Luke took her hand in his and kissed it ever so softly. Emma smiled. No matter what, she could always count on Luke. He was at every performance, club, vacation, event, or holiday where she needed him. He was so reliable. Right now, he locked eyes with her as if to say, "I know your dad couldn't make it, but I'm here and always will be."

Luke didn't disappoint her. Throughout the course of the night, he went out of his way to be more affectionate, make her laugh and smile, and make her feel special as only he could. They sat on the porch under a full, beautiful moon, enjoying the coolness of the night and snuggling for warmth. He pushed the porch swing lazily back and forth. "Hey, my girl." Emma smiled up at him. She loved it when he called her that. "I saved something special for last." Emma looked up curiously. He pulled out a small box. Emma opened it tenderly, even dreaming for just a moment that it was a ring. However, the box was too big.

She opened it and gasped, "Oh Luke!" Inside was a stunning sterling silver necklace with real diamonds and a pink, accented heart with her name written across it. "Oh, Luke," she said again. "It's wonderful."

"Right away when I saw it, I thought, *Oh, this is so Emma. She'll love it.* The only problem was making sure they had your name, which they did. Here, let me put it on."

Emma leaned forward, letting Luke drape the smooth, cold metal over her delicate, white skin. He fastened it and then pulled her back against him. He folded his arms around her. Emma touched the charm with her slender fingers. She knew she would cherish it forever. Reaching for him, she turned and moved her graceful fingers along his face. She traced his strong chin and his smooth cheeks. A fire lit up inside them, and he reached for her. Smoothing out her hair with his fingers, he tilted her head toward his and gently pressed his smooth lips against hers. Emma responded to his warm breath with a deep kiss of her own. She let out a low gasp as the kiss deepened.

He pulled her closer onto his lap and continued to kiss her. They didn't stop, letting their love flow between them. Emma pushed herself solidly against him and wrapped her arms tighter around him. She clung to him. So soft and sweet were his kisses, she thought she would never release him.

After a while, the couple settled back in swinging and holding on to one another tightly. Neither knew what was happening, and neither thought about anything but the present moment. That was how they lived, moment to moment, clinging to each other's love. The future wasn't far off, but they seemed unaware how far they were drifting.

Emma was finally forced to go into the house after Luke left. Though she had wanted to linger on the porch, the night air had become too chilly to face without him. She was kind of glad at the moment that her dad hadn't been able to make it. She might have spent the whole night with him instead of experiencing it with Luke. Besides, she knew her dad was going to make it up to her. How, she didn't know, but she was filled with anticipation about what he might plan. What to do now? She couldn't sleep anyway, and Luke was driving. She'd text Jordyn back.

Her friend had texted her, "Happy birthday," but she hadn't taken time to respond. Now she couldn't wait to tell her about Luke's gift and about her special night, minus some of the more private details.

"Hey, Jordyn, sorry I didn't respond right away. Mom made me dinner—my favorite pasta and smothered mushroom chicken. Thanks. I really had fun tonight. You'll never guess what Luke got me. It was so sweet."

"What?!" Jordyn texted back.

"He got me a necklace with my name written in it. Can u believe it? It looks expensive 2, lol."

"Awesome. Can't wait 2 c."

"He is so romantic! He's trying to make up for my dad being gone. He told me I was the most beautiful girl he had ever laid eyes on ... What a line. He's just awesome like that."

"Yeah, you're really lucky, although he's a little on the boring side."

"What! Not uh. He snuggled me on the front porch all evening, saying sweet things to me."

"Yeah, really romantic, but not exciting. I want someone who makes life fun."

"Of course, fun would be your priority, Jordyn."

"Yeah, well I'm sick of boring."

"Are we talking about the same person? Your life is never boring."

"Seeeee? All the more reason for him to be fun. We've got to be compatible, you know."

"Okay, I'll be on the lookout for a fun guy whose nonromantic."

"I didn't say nonromantic. I said he has to be fun."

"Okay, fun with a little romance on the side lol. C ya tomorrow."

"Oh yeah, English class. Fun …"

Emma laughed, closing her phone. The class wasn't so bad, but apparently, fun was the new standard in Jordyn's life.

Work didn't let up, and with school around the corner, the scholarship race became even more intense. Except for Josh, of course, who knew his dad would cover any necessary expenses, the interns seemed on edge. Kate became more worried by the day. Eliza was also concerned but couldn't imagine her mom letting her go home, even if she didn't get the scholarship. However, she didn't want her mom taking out a second job or something like that, so she continued to work hard. The two avoided conversation with Josh but were never rude.

Annie proved to be everything everyone imagined her to be. She was friendly and the writers loved working with her. Stephanie had also taken on a new role. She scouted the company's competition and worked on new ideas for their publishing magazine. Unfortunately, Kate, Eliza, and the majority of them were still editing. However, everyone's work was not of the same quality, and Mr. Grant had pointed out Eliza's thoroughness several times. She hoped that meant that she would be awarded a scholarship, but wasn't sure. In addition to work, she had started socially hanging out with many of the interns. They enjoyed each other's company, and the least competitive of the group started helping critique each other's assignments to make them better.

Chapter 6

The week flew by for Emma: more projects, more homework. Before she knew it, it was Saturday again. She and Luke had taken the day for themselves. They went to miniature golf, the park, lunch, the museum, and finally dinner at Patricia's Pasta House. Cheesy name but really good food. Now it was six o'clock and they were running out of things to do.

"Hey, Emma …"

"Yeah?"

"What do you want to do? I mean, dinner was fabulous, but we still have some time before I have to take you home."

"We could see a movie or something."

"No, I feel like doing something else."

"Like what?"

"I don't know. Do you want to go for a drive, my sweet one?"

"Sure. That sounds kind of romantic."

"You first, milady." Emma hopped into the car and looked at Luke. His tall frame filled up the whole window. After shutting her door, he walked around and crawled into the driver's seat.

"Luke, I really love you."

Smiling down at her, he took her hand in his and kissed it. "Me too, *mi amor.*" He had taken to calling her "amor," since that was the one word he had learned out of his three years of Spanish class. That and *"Tengo hambre,"* meaning, "I'm hungry." Oh boys. They always had only two things on their minds.

Luke interrupted her thoughts by saying, "Emma, have you ever thought about what's next after high school?"

"Yeah, college, silly."

"No, I mean us."

Emma tried not to stare at him. She forced herself to breath. How many times had she rehearsed this very conversation in her head? Now she didn't want to mess it up. Maybe Luke had better start first. "Okay, what do you think about us?"

"Emma, I don't know. I've thought about this a lot." Emma's heart fluttered. So he did think about them. "I love you. I feel like I could never leave you, but I'm going to California on a full-ride scholarship. I don't have much choice, but somehow, I can't dare let you go." Tenderly, he glanced at her and then redirected his attention to the open road. Emma gathered all her courage. She was finally hearing what she longed to hear. After a year and a half of dating, he was finally discussing where their relationship was headed.

"You mean like never let me go? Like getting married?" Her voice came out barely audible.

"I don't want to rush. I still need to finish school, but yes, I can't believe I'm saying this, but yes. Forever. I can't lose you, Emma. You mean everything to me." He gave her hand a tight squeeze. Emma brightened and leaned over the center console to plant a large kiss on his cheek.

She whispered seductively "Then you won't. Perhaps I'll get a full ride to UC."

Throwing his free arm around her, he replied, "I like the sound of that." He pulled off on the side of the road.

"Where are we going?"

"Somewhere where I can kiss you crazy."

They found the perfect spot right after they pulled off. Down the street, there was an abandoned parking lot that overlooked a small creek. He maneuvered into a spot beneath the spreading willow tree, which offered a sense of privacy. Before she knew it, Luke had her in her arms kissing her. Her heart soared. He loved her, and he would love her always. Her fingers dug into his back and caressed his face. She finally had to pull back because the console in between them was causing her some discomfort.

"Wanna go on a walk?" he suggested, leading her out.

Walking hand in hand, they started talking, for the first time, about their future together. Finally, tired they sat under the shade of an oak tree.

"How far did we walk?" she asked breathlessly.

"I don't know, but I'm too tired to walk that far back again."

Emma's eyes shone as she looked at her sweetheart. He cuddled her and started to kiss her neck. Emma blushed and turned around to kiss him back. His arms, strong and muscular, held her close. Emma breathed in the smell of him. She could smell his amazing cologne and hear his heartbeat. She could smell the sweetness of the grass and trees surrounding her. Excitement and passion overtook them both as they embraced. Without realizing what they were doing they crossed boundaries they had never crossed before. Their passion for each other seemed to make decisions for them. One thing led to another and then the special moment was over.

When it ended, Emma was still reeling from their encounter. To her, it was a moment that promised that he would love her forever. For him, it was a moment he hadn't planned but didn't regret.

The Hope of Eliza

Slowly getting up, she brushed herself off. He smiled. Suddenly shy, Emma glanced around. The shyness faded when he pulled into a tight hug.

"Wow, you are beautiful," he whispered. "Are you okay? You don't regret it, do you?"

"No, never. It was amazing."

Smiling, he took her hand, and they walked back to the car. Emma had never felt this way before. Luke went to amazing lengths to make sure she was okay, both emotionally and physically. Though it had hurt slightly, it being her first time and all, there was still an unexplainable pleasure about it. She had shared a part of herself that she had never shared with anyone before. Her body and emotions were spent, but in a good way.

Not until they were in the car still smiling did Luke say, "Oh crap." And then he looked embarrassed.

"What? What's wrong?"

"Nothing." But his face had turned a deep shade of red.

Emma didn't know what to say. She had never seen his face so red. "Just tell me."

"We didn't … Um, well, I wasn't planning on … We probably should have used some sort of protection."

Emma burst out loud laughing. It was an overflow of her emotions, one she couldn't explain.

"What's so funny?"

"Nothing," Emma said, trying to regain some control. "I'm on birth control, remember? You know how bad I cramp without them. We're fine."

Luke relaxed visibly. "Are you sure you haven't missed any pills?"

"No. I'm careful, Luke." He smiled and looked at her again.

How could he be such an idiot? He almost endangered them. He hadn't even given a thought to protection a moment ago. He could kick himself for not protecting them. How many times had his guy friends told him to always carry one? How could he be so stupid? Perhaps because she was so beautiful. Her skin glistened, dancing in the sun, and her face seemed to shine. Her curves and the softness of her skin drew him even now. Well, it wouldn't happen again. Next time, he'd make sure that they were protected. Sure, she was on birth control, but this was his responsibility. She was his responsibility. He didn't want to hurt her. Looking over at her now, she was on cloud nine. But would she stay that way? He silently prayed he hadn't made a really big mistake. There was no denying what he now knew to be 100 percent true. She had never given herself to anyone. Anyone besides him, that is.

Somehow, his possessiveness toward her seemed to grow. He would protect her at all costs. She was his now, and he wanted her forever. Wow, she was amazing. Luke had never been with someone who so eagerly loved him. Every action, every move of her body, emitted pent-up passion, like she had been waiting for him this whole time. Pride swelled through him. He would never regret that moment as long as he lived, so long as she didn't.

Eliza sat across from two people who were fast becoming her closest friends. She laughed cavalierly as Danny slipped into his impersonation of Mr. Grant. "Now students, this is a huuuuuuuge opportunity." The way he emphasized "huge opportunity" sounded just like Mr. Grant causing the girls to burst out laughing. Danny wasn't so much making fun of Mr. Grant as he was having fun impersonating him.

"You should show Mr. Grant your talent," beamed an amused Kate.

"Yeah, I don't know how he'd take it," Danny replied with a smile still on his face.

"I think he'd be fine. He has a sense of humor," Eliza reassured. They all burst out laughing.

"You should go for it. Danny, I'd love to see the look on his face either way," Kate teased.

Eliza drifted away for a moment. Danny was good-looking. She wouldn't quite go as far as hot, but his personality seemed to add to his looks.

Danny was funny and kind. He was down to earth and would talk to or hang out with anyone. His unique vantage on writing and reporting often silenced the most efficient argument. His way with words was penetrating, but also disarming. She guessed humor had a way of making an audience at ease. Danny always said you never had to water down the truth if you could first appeal to your audience. Eliza wasn't quite sure of that herself, yet it did make sense. Danny's articles had a way of befriending his audience. It was as if the article was a civil discussion about the facts rather than a throw-it-in-your-face piece. He truly had talent. His style allowed him to report on hot-button issues, without leaving an insulted audience.

In addition to that, his stocky frame, amazing smile, athletic build, and wavy, brown, thick hair made him a stellar candidate for reporting. He was considering that field. This internship was a chance to strengthen his writing. Reporters never grew out of that field, he had said.

"Earth to Eliza."

"Oh, sorry, guys."

"We're leaving," Kate added.

"Okay, what about the check?"

"Mr. Casanova over here already took care of it."

"Danny," Eliza scolded.

"No, really. I wanted to, and I'm living off of a little more than an intern's paycheck." Danny's father owned his own company and Danny handled the website and did some online work for him in his spare time. But still, Eliza thought it was overly generous, considering they weren't on a date or anything. They were just all hanging out. Still, it was nice, considering her current situation. "Thanks, Danny. That was really sweet."

Danny smiled and shrugged.

"We don't want to go back yet, right?" whined Kate hugging to Eliza's arm.

"Well, we should get to work on that article."

"Come on, Eliza. Where's your sense of procrastination? Let's take a walk to digest all that food," Danny joined in. The pleading in his blue eyes was ridiculously irresistible.

Eliza rolled her eyes. "Okay, just a few minutes. We eventually have to get back."

Danny joined arms with the two girls as they headed down the street toward all the downtown shops.

Emma couldn't sleep. Wow, he had finally told her! She had felt it all along. Luke really wanted her, as in forever! Boy, did he prove it to her. Emma remembered fondly how he had made love to her. His lips had felt like something she craved for. Their hunger couldn't be stopped. Ever so gently had he made love to her. Every movement gentle and sure. He loved her. She hadn't meant for it to happen, nor had he, but oh, how good it felt to know he loved her.

By now, her virginity was evident to him, if it hadn't been before. He was her first and last on this earth. How happy she was that he sealed their love, never to be broken. They were made for each other. Soon, they would belong together. Flittingly, she wondered if Luke would consider marriage before he finished college. She thought not, but what did it really matter? Eventually, they would be together forever.

Emma sat up. She still hungered for his affection. From what she heard, things just got better from here, but Emma was unsure that that could be true. Already she wanted to call him back. She pictured herself sneaking him upstairs and just lying in her bed together, his strong arm supporting her head. *Emma, go to sleep*, she commanded herself, but she couldn't. Her excitement showed on her face. Instead, she got up and journaled and spent the rest of the night texting Luke. They flirted and talked about forever.

She asked him if they were going to do this again. "Of course," he said, "but I'm not in a hurry." He didn't want their parents finding out. They would just feel bad about it. "Besides, we have a whole year before we're off to college. There will be plenty of freedom there." At one point, he asked about how she felt about them making love.

"Were you not listening when you were making love to me? I said this was all I wanted."

To which he responded "Perhaps I was a little distracted."

Chapter 7

Eliza wanted to scream. She had been at this first assignment for five days straight. She wanted to succeed in this program. She wanted to do her best and come out on top. She wasn't worried about her qualifications; she could do the job, and she could do it well. The problem wasn't the difficulty but the competitive nature of the program. The pressure was extreme. Every day, she worried about her communication. She needed to communicate her professionalism, her strong work ethic, capability, responsibility, and most important, her potential. Liza worked on these things daily, competing for the scholarship, and then for a job or at least a great recommendation. The problem was what she called shining moments. It wasn't enough just doing the right things; you had to be caught doing the right things. Shining moments were the moments where she got to display her talent to those in charge. These moments were priceless, and one unfocussed moment was an irreplaceable opportunity to impress. She knew she could do it.

I just need a cheerleader, she thought.

So far from home, her thoughts turned to Grammy and Mom—the two constants in her life. Friends had come and gone, but they had never left. Lifting the phone, she chose to call Mom. She needed her love, but also her instruction. It was great to have a mom who loved and supported her. Not everyone was so blessed. Her mom thought her daughter had limitless potential and value. She could go anywhere and accomplish anything. Only time would tell if that was true, Eliza thought as she speed-dialed her dear mother.

Grammy happened to be with her, which was perfect, because after talking with them both, she felt reenergized and refocused. She would need both energy and focus to attack this story.

───※───

"I'm glad we decided to do this."

"Yeah, me too." Eliza pushed her sunglasses back to keep the hair out of her face; she was nervous. They both were. Tomorrow, Mr. Grant would announce his decision about the scholarships. She could feel the tension mounting in the office. More than one stable intern had had a meltdown the last few days. Eliza had done her best, but even small mistakes seemed to be too much to handle. Eliza wondered, *Because I worked in my room instead of the office, does it seem like I'm not committed? If I run five minutes late, is that my last strike? Have I taken too many bathroom breaks to be considered a professional?* Okay, that last one hadn't really crossed her mind, but that was how she felt. She felt as if at any moment she could be kicked to the side because of something she couldn't control. She felt hopeless and a bit deflated. Her usual upbeat personality had taken a hit. Another something that could get her name tossed out of the running? Yes, it was good to be out of the office. Eliza glanced in the little boutique.

"Hey, Kate, do you mind if we stop in here for a minute? I think I see something my mom would like." Knowing Kate's answer, she headed into the small shop filled with many delicate figurines. The tiny bell over the door chimed as she walked through. A young woman greeted her and asked if she needed any help finding something. "No thanks. Just looking." *At least until I find a price tag somewhere,* she thought.

Eliza moved across the floor as Kate entered. She was drawn to a tiny ballerina whose face looked so angelic it could have been part of the nativity scene. She was dressed in a flowing satin material, with just a trace of sparkle. Of course, it was pink. Her mother would love it. It was priced for $19.99. Twenty dollars may not have seemed like a lot to anyone else, but to Eliza, it was a little difficult to swallow. Oh well. No matter how she had to make this work, it would be well worth the sacrifice. The lady at the counter checked her out and carefully wrapped the doll in tissue and then placed it in a sturdy box. Eliza thanked her and they continued their shopping excursion.

Even though their shopping trip only landed them one more purchase—an ice-cream cone—it had served its purpose to relax and distract.

"Emma, aren't you coming down for breakfast?"

Emma jumped up with a start. When had she fallen asleep? What time was it? Picking up her phone, she looked at the last text. "Can't wait to be with u, baby. I'll call you tomorrow." She had fallen asleep on their conversation. The time on the last text showed 3:45 a.m.

"Good morning," she texted him. But it was already twelve.

"I'll be down in one minute, Mom."

"Hey, sweetheart, you look sleepy. Wow, twelve o'clock. That's a new record even for you on a Sunday morning."

"Yeah, I must have been tired. I slept like a rock."

"An almost-deaf rock, I should say." Her mother smiled. "Dad and I already ate. He was sad he didn't get to say hi. He had to run to the office. I have no idea when to expect him back. I thought I'd heat you up some French toast and make you some eggs before I leave for my spa appointment. Want to come? I'm sure they could fit you in."

"No thanks. I've got to finish up some schoolwork before tomorrow. Have fun though."

"Okay, stay out of trouble," she said jokingly.

Emma smiled. Trouble might be what she was aiming for.

That night, Eliza didn't sleep well. When she got up in the morning, she remembered tossing and turning, but no sleep. Frankly, she wasn't surprised. Her stomach was in knots. Rolling out of bed, she decided a cold shower might be the answer to start the day with a jolt. After that, she made herself a pot of coffee, and made sure she picked out something decent to where. Goodness, this wasn't like her. Usually, she was confident and sure of herself. Today, she had grave doubts.

Though she knew the decision had already been made, she said a quick prayer that all the interns would handle things gracefully and that no one would have to leave.

Arriving at the office earlier than usual, Eliza got out of her car and headed upstairs to her desk.

Shifting her balance, she looked around nonchalantly. The office was buzzing and people were chatting quietly, but something felt odd. She looked around the room. Jim was in the corner talking to Stephanie, whose bright smile and gorgeous laugh could be spotted from a mile away. Danny stared intently at his computer. Kate wasn't here yet. Only Annie looked up. "Hey, Eliza. Kate came in a few hours ago and left a note on your desk. She looked surprised that anyone was here so early, but I had to get a head start today. Anyway, I assured her that I'd make sure you got it."

"Do you know what it's about?"

"No ... I mean I'm assuming she's sick and just wanted to let you know she won't be here today." Eliza walked over to her desk started her computer.

It was odd she didn't just call. No sense in coming all the way down here if she was feeling ill. Come to think of it, she could have just walked across the hall in the dorms. Letting her purse slide to the floor, she read her friend's note.

Dear Liza,

You have been such a friend to me, my only friend. I don't know why you have been so kind to me. My days at this office, spent next to you, have been so pleasant. Even with those two lovebirds pleasantly and annoyingly laughing together. It'll be interesting for you to see if that goes anywhere, which brings me to my main point.

I wasn't picked for the scholarship; I can't stay. I couldn't face you with this terrible news in person. Send everyone my regards, except Josh, of course. I just thought I should let you know how much you really meant to me as a supporter, encourager, and cheerleader. Your maturity and strength have impressed me almost as much as your joy and constant smile.

I used to look at myself in the mirror after a horrible night's sleep, my plain, dark hair messed and tangled, and picture a memory I have of you. You waltzed into the office, your smile bright and playful, flipping my ponytail as you walked by. You said, "Oooh, someone's got soft hair," and then jokingly you added, "What shampoo do you use? I need to get some of that." I don't know why that thought crosses my mind at those moments, but it does. I can picture you in your light-gray business suit with the top cut in the most recent style and the light-pink long-sleeve shirt. I'll always be able to picture you like that. Somehow, I know that picture will always stay with me no matter what happens.

Love, Kate

An alarmed look passed over Eliza's face as a sinking feeling rooted itself in her gut. Kate was rarely sentimental. Though they were good friends, this letter sounded nothing like her, yet it was in her handwriting. Why not say good-bye properly? Too hard in person? Eliza didn't buy it.

She gathered her things and touched her speed dial. "Kate, pick up," she demanded. When it went to voicemail, she called again. With no answer the second time, she rushed to her car. She didn't know how to explain it, but she couldn't shake the feeling that Kate was saying good-bye for good.

Chapter 8

Luke didn't come over, but they did talk on the phone for several hours. He promised to see her at school. She could hardly wait. It was like a new door had been opened. Never had she felt so sure of their relationship or assured that Luke meant every word that he said. She spent her hours Googling the college they would go to, the married dorms, and the places to see. She had it all planned out. She couldn't wait for the promising future.

Luke loved her!

Occasionally, small feelings of guilt crept up, but she was quick to drown them with happy thoughts of a perfect future. She imagined herself more mature and ready to handle an adult relationship with adult responsibilities. She couldn't wait till they graduated. Maybe over spring break their parents would let them drive down to the college together. Hey, that was a thought. She couldn't wait to suggest it to Luke on Monday.

Emma smiled shyly as Luke walked down to the hall toward her. Man, she could feel the heat setting her cheeks aflame. *Oh, dear,* she thought. *If I don't stop smiling like an idiot people will know for sure.*

"You look beautiful!"

Emma was wearing a cute sundress with high heels. Her makeup was flawlessly done and emphasized her beautiful blue eyes. Her hair fell down to her shoulders in very loose curls that resembled waves. Her dangling earrings added the perfect touch.

"Hi," she said, blushing again.

"Emma," he said as he laughed, "Why are you so red?"

Emma playfully slapped him on the arm. "I am not," she retorted.

"Yes, yes, I do believe you are, milady."

"Hey, guys, what did I miss?"

"Nothing, Jordyn," Emma said.

"Well, it sure looks like I've missed something," she retorted.

"Nothing. Luke just got here."

"All right. Well, perhaps I have something for you, then. Are you going to Tyler Pearson's party?"

Emma looked to Luke, who shrugged. "Maybe."

"Well, you have to. This is going to be *the* party of senior year. You have to be there to protect your social reputations. Besides, a best friend could get rather lonely without your being there."

"I thought Mason invited you to go with him," Emma said playfully.

"So he did, Ms. Know-It-All, but I still need someone there to keep my feet on the ground."

"Literally," Emma said.

Jordyn shot her friend a piercing glance. "I'll behave," she insisted.

"Yeah, stick with Mason. He's a good guy. He'll keep you out of trouble," Luke interjected.

"Thanks, Brother Luke, but I can handle myself. I assure you," Jordyn defended.

Luke tipped his baseball cap in mock gentleman behavior and said, "Okay, milady." Then he added, "Maybe we should come along, Em. That girl might need us."

Jordyn gasped, "Ha ha, Luke Howard. Like you could keep me out of trouble. Trouble is your middle name."

He only smiled. "See you ladies at lunch."

Emma smiled too. Her two best friends got along very well, even if Jordyn could have her moments.

Luke had, in fact, bailed her out before, but perhaps she was too drunk to remember. Luke wasn't a troublemaker, as Jordyn claimed; he was a very decent guy who she just happened to be falling hopelessly in love with.

Kate looked from the mirror and back at herself. There were no longer any tears. Sometimes, tears couldn't mend broken hearts or stamp out the hopelessness that overtook someone's life. Completely useless, tears were. Now there was nothing but cold, hard, desperate resolve in the face of the one who stared back at her in the mirror. A small voice whispered, "That's not you," but she chose to drown that voice because this was all that was left of her. She had run out of options. She had fought desperately, trying to find the will to live. Now, this was the only way to drown the pain. She would not do this to punish others. Though maybe then her family would ... No, it was a desperate attempt to end the pain that kept mounting inside her. Death was the only way to freedom, or so she thought. She swore nothing else could take the pain away.

From childhood, her life had been riddled with pain. The scared little girl hiding in the corner still lived inside her. The fighting was still etched into her brain. She could repeat every argument, every angry word. The cursing and yelling were all routine. But occasionally, it would escalate to more than that. Physical abuse was the least of her worries. At first, Kate hadn't wanted to see her parents split up, but by junior high, she began to see it as the only way out. However, things only got worse. As bad as Dad had been, Mom was worse. Now, she was highly depressed, never home, and always found fault in the oldest of her children: Kate. As if drugs and alcohol weren't enough, there were the men. Kate thought that this might pull her mother out of a drowning abyss, but she was wrong.

Kate spent her life trying to shield her younger two siblings from Mom's abuse. Sure, physically Mom's slaps were nothing compared to what they'd lived through, but emotionally, her mother had the capacity to destroy every precious ounce of life left inside of her children. Her manipulation and guilt trips and blame games all took a toll on the three little lives that she should have been caring for.

Kate would confront her mother and try to reason with her when she was sober. It never did any good. No change was ever made until that fateful day. Though physical abuse was hard on a child, at thirteen, to be the sexual victim of a man was a million times worse. Kate thought that everything good inside her had shriveled up and died that day.

The Hope of Eliza

After it was over, Robby, only eleven at the time, knew something had gone wrong behind those closed doors. He tried to comfort her the only way he knew how, which was to hold her and cry himself.

And that was how Mom found them hours later when she asked where Hank was. Though Kate had felt so ashamed, she had finally realized that good might still come from the situation. She sent her little brother out of the room and told her mother every last nasty detail about Hank.

Her mother's reaction surprised her.

She was irate, but not at Hank. "How dare you make up cruel stories to haunt me just so that I will leave Hank! You never wanted me to be happy. You little selfish brat! I'm sick of your lies. You'd better get away from me before I kill you! Just go."

But she wouldn't. No matter what had happened to her, she wouldn't leave them. Finally, at sixteen, she got a job and made a plan to leave. She succeeded in slipping out in the middle of the night with her siblings and provided for them as best as she could for about a year. Life was still hard but rather peaceful, until the police showed up and took them away. Someone at school had noticed her sibling's lack of food and new clothes, but instead of the help they desperately needed, they got split up. Kate went to a group home and her siblings went to two different families. Her mother's rights were terminated once they heard Kate's testimony, completely ending any small hope of reconciliation with her mother.

If life wasn't bad enough at that point, Josh humiliated her and left her, making her finally and completely all alone. But at nineteen, she had been given a break: this job, this opportunity for a scholarship and a real future. She had made something of herself, and she was going to adopt her siblings. Until yesterday, when she got the news that Robby was in juvenile hall, and her sister was being adopted. Now, she had nothing left, nothing to live for. "I have rights," she had argued with the social worker. No, it turned out she didn't, because she wasn't in a financial position to provide child care for Carolina and wasn't that much older than Robby. In addition to all this, she didn't get the scholarship, which meant her opportunity to make something of herself had vanished. Mr. Grant had been kind enough to tell her in person last night that she wouldn't be receiving the scholarship. When she had asked why, he said simply, "There were too many deserving. I hope you can stay on."

Stay on. Stay on? This was the only life she had. With no way to go to school and no way to afford to stay here, even with the six-hundred-dollar supplement, she would have to leave her only home: this tiny dorm room. She could only take out a student loan with this internship because

The Hope of Eliza

of the small income it provided, but without the scholarship, the loan wouldn't be enough for school. Furthermore, her stipend was only good if she took full-time classes, which she currently couldn't afford without a parent signature for additional loans. There was no other alternative.

Holding a picture of the two most beloved people in the world, she did the only thing she knew how to. She had said good-bye to Eliza and to her siblings, explaining that it wasn't their fault.

Looking into the mirror, she grabbed the pill bottles and forced herself to take every last one. Falling onto her pillow, she held onto the picture as if for dear life, which was kind of ironic, she thought, because she was dying.

Fifteen minutes went by, and she was getting drowsy. She started hearing the thudding of her heart in her dream, but then she heard shouting—hysterical shouting, as if her heart were screaming in agony. Only the agony was not her own. It was Liza's as she banged furiously on the door.

The next days passed peacefully for Emma. Senior year was a blast. So many easy filler classes because she had never ever failed a class in her life. Fun, fun, fun. Senior prank planning, senior ditch day, senior service day, school dances that suddenly everyone attended because it was there last chance to have this high school experience. Prom was already the talk of the school. The juniors were rumored to have planned something spectacular. They had even been fundraising outside of school to make the event a sure success. Generous benefactors had contributed serious money. Already, the budget for prom had more than doubled. Emma's life wasn't showing signs of slowing down. Already into the second semester of their last year, time seemed to be flying. Jordyn and the girls, including Emma, had gone shopping for what promised to be the party of a lifetime.

Arriving home, she flung all her shopping bags onto her bed: there was the shoe bag, the sexy-little-dress-for-the-party bag, the accessories bag from Claire's, the purse bag, and the I-just-wanted-a-few-more-shirts-and-pairs-of-shoes-while-I'm-at-it bag. Luke would have been laughing at the numerous bags taking up her entire bed. Tyler's party was two days from now and all she could think about was going with Luke. Maybe they too could find a comfy make-out spot for a change. *Who says Jordyn should have all the fun?*

―――――――

Eliza breathed heavily. "Open up!" Her voice betrayed her deep emotion. "Please, Kate, open the door."

Frantically, she banged harder. She couldn't stop her heart from beating. The adrenaline coursed through her body. Never once did she question herself. She could've been wrong. Kate might not have even been in the room. She could be creating ruckus for no reason. Not once did she ponder how this might look to anyone else. It was like she knew. "Kate, I know you are in there! If you don't open the door, I'm going to bust it down."

Kate heard a voice in the distance. *Am I dying?* she thought. But the voice was Eliza's. Eliza was here. Why?

She let out a moan. She could just sit back and this would all be over. Even though she was on the verge of unconsciousness, she felt so drawn to her friend. For the first time, she had a glimmer of hope that life might be worth living again, for reasons she couldn't explain. Someone loved her; Eliza knew. She knew she was dying, and she cared.

She pushed herself up but collapsed back onto the bed. "Eliza," she whispered, her voice barely audible. She tried to move again, but couldn't. Kate glanced at the white ceiling, the last thing she saw before she slipped away.

Eliza was becoming more panicked by the second. She thought she heard something inside. That was all the encouragement she needed. She had no idea if she could muster up the strength, but without thought, she kicked the door. Undeterred when it didn't budge, she kicked a few more times. Bursting through the door with strength she didn't know she possessed, she saw Kate lying on the bed unconscious.

She dialed 911. Rushing to her side, she dropped to her knees automatically, checking for a pulse. "Yes, I need an ambulance. My friend is down. I think … I think she might have tried to commit suicide."

Chapter 9

Emma hung up the phone. Boys! They could be your heroes one minute and your broken heart the next.

Luke was getting nervous about the party. Apparently, talk had become so big the administration "might" have gotten word of it. Might have. Luke was now worried about his basketball season. He didn't want to get suspended by being caught at some party. Some party, indeed. Why did Luke have to get so noble all of a sudden? He drank and partied along with the rest of them. He was just scared, and now, he was putting her in a position of having to go without him or not going at all. She was so frustrated. She had planned for weeks about what she would wear and what they would do and now he was going to disappoint her. He had tried to make up for it by saying they could spend the evening together. It wasn't the same. It was her senior year too. Didn't her opinion matter?

She hugged her knees to her chest, while sitting on her bed. She choked back a sob. How could he be so selfish?

The last few minutes had passed in a blur. The EMTs moved in so fast, Eliza could only stand by helplessly looking on. The EMTs quickly loaded her friend on a stretcher. Eliza followed the ambulance in her car. When it accelerated way past the speed limit, she forced herself to slow down. *You can't do anything if you end up in a ditch*, she thought. She started praying.

After reaching the hospital, she parked and ran inside the building. She saw a reception lady who was nicely dressed and sitting calmly behind her desk. "Can I help you?" the lady asked.

"Yes, I need an update on Kate. Last name Beckett. She just came in via ambulance."

Searching the computer, the lady slowly shook her head. "I'm sorry. No new information. They brought her in to the ICU."

Though Eliza was a little frustrated by the lack of news, she was at least relieved to know that Kate was still alive. At least the woman hadn't said she'd been taken to the morgue. She sighed. What a nightmare.

She dialed her mother. Urging her to pray, she told the whole story. She felt so alone. Her mother said she would drive up, but Eliza told her to hold off because she was fine for now. After hanging up, she just sat there. The minutes seemed to go by slowly.

A handsome, young police officer entered the hospital. Fully armed and with short, blond hair, he had an easy gait about him. He looked around and then walked up to Eliza. "Hello, ma' am. I was wondering if I could ask you a few questions."

Eliza wasn't afraid of the law; she hadn't done anything wrong ... Unless you count the whole breaking and entering thing, but that might have saved her. Might have. "Sure." She got up and followed him to the corner.

"I just need to know the details about this evening," he said calmly.

"I received a weird letter from her, and I just knew. I felt like she was going to do something to herself. I tried to call her and went to her house. Her door was locked, and I knocked on it. I didn't hear anything at first. Then I heard a soft sound and knew she was inside. I got in and found her lying there. I didn't know what happened, but I called 911."

"Do you still have that note?"

Eliza thought hard. "Yes ... it's in my car, I believe. Do you need me to get it?"

"It's not necessary right now, but can you sum up what she said? Where did you find the letter?"

Eliza relayed all the details she could remember. The police officer thanked her and then left.

Sighing, she sank back into her seat. The emotions of the morning seemed to catch up with her. She tried to stop them, but now the tears freely flowed. She busied herself by texting her mom and playing Free Cell. Finally, a doctor approached her. "Are you here to see about a Kate Beckett?"

"Yes," Eliza said hurriedly. She rose to her feet.

"I'm very sorry, but I have to ask if you are a relative. I can't release any information about patients who aren't relatives, you understand."

Eliza dropped her gaze. "I'm all she has right now," she said, her voice trembling. Dabbing her eyes, she looked up.

The doctor smiled sympathetically. "I see. When she is coherent enough, I'll ask her if she wants to see her sister. Is that right?"

Smiling, Eliza nodded. "Yes, thank you, doctor."

"Well, she is very lucky to be alive. Thanks to you, I have heard. We had to pump her stomach. She had apparently been trying to die. She swallowed a whole large bottle of strong pain medication. Several more minutes, and we wouldn't have been able to bring her back. With that being said, I don't know if she wants to be alive. Some people who have tried to commit suicide are often angry at first that they are still alive. However, she's young. I think she'll get over it. She's stable now, still really groggy. We have her in ICU to keep a close eye on her.

"I'll be out in a bit. You hang tight. It'll be a little while if you need to take care of anything. Maybe go home and change." He nodded to her slacks. "She'll be in the ICU for a little while. Someone is sitting with her, so you have no need to worry."

Eliza nodded.

The doctor disappeared through the doors. She would go home and change, maybe even shower. She also needed to call her mom and her work. They were probably worried. Worried or irate. No way to tell unless she called him. She had Mr. Grant's cell number in case of emergencies. Eliza guessed this would qualify. However, she didn't know how much of Kate's personal life she wanted to reveal. Perhaps she would just say Kate was in the hospital. After all, no one else knew what the note had said.

<hr />

"Yes! Thanks, baby. That means so much to me. Are you sure it'll be okay? I don't want you to get in trouble. Okay." She hung up her cell phone, practically jumping up and down.

"Yes! He said he would go. This means we can ..." Emma covered her mouth. Her thoughts struck her before she even had a chance to think them. She wanted to have be with Luke, again. That was what she had truly been wanting. It had nothing to do with the party. That's why she had been so disappointed. She had hoped they could steal a few moments alone at the party. She began to see it all in her mind: her own love story transformed into a passionate love scene. This time, they wouldn't have to stop.

Just as quickly as she dreamed what it would be like to have him hold her again, another thought flitted into her mind. Now that she thought about it, she felt ... guilty? No, she didn't regret it. She didn't.

Emma couldn't admit, even to herself, that she sometimes felt guilty that they had been together. She couldn't describe why though. It wasn't as if she thought it was wrong. She did feel bad about keeping it from her mother, but she would never tell her. Perhaps that's why she felt bad. Yeah, that was the only reason. It had to be. And since she was already keeping it to herself, why not enjoy some well-deserved time with Luke?

Yep, everything looked like it was back on track.

The Hope of Eliza

Eliza was nervous. The doctor had said Kate wanted to see her. She hoped that was really true. Could it be possible that she still really wished that she had died? *I mean, it could have just been a depressing day.* The suicide attempt—she couldn't believe she was able to label this terrible tragedy—could have just been a rushed bad mistake, right? *I mean, no one, surely not my best friend, wants to end her life forever.* Could she have been planning this? Could Eliza have been blind to any signs? *I guess that's what everyone who is close to someone who makes that choice ends up thinking. What could I have done?*

Eliza tried to comfort herself with the truth that this wasn't her fault, that she couldn't have prevented this. But knowing that fact didn't make it any easier. It didn't take away her guilt. Logically, she knew she couldn't blame herself, but this wasn't a logical situation. It was an emotional one. And her emotions betrayed her by defying all reason. They insisted that she could have done something. Pushing her feelings aside, for the moment, Eliza tried to concentrate.

Eliza would give Kate the scholarship, if that was what it took. Which, come to think of it, she hadn't been awarded yet, or maybe she had, but just didn't know. Funny thing was it no longer meant that much to her, especially because it had contributed to Kate's horrible situation. What would Mr. Grant say if he could see her now? What did it matter? Perhaps he could have heard her out about her need for the scholarship, but in the end, Eliza knew deep down inside that Kate—even if Eliza didn't want to think about it—had made her own choice.

Eliza bravely pushed the door to Kate's room open. She saw Kate lying on the white hospital bed. She looked awful and weak. She didn't smile or even try to sit up. Her gaze was focused somewhere else.

"Hey, how are you feeling?" Eliza managed, as if she was merely visiting a friend who was sick.

Kate took one look at Eliza and burst into tears. "I'm sorry ... I'm so sorry."

Eliza left her purse on a chair and went to her friend, holding her while she wept, but Kate was only able to say those few words over and over again. "I'm sorry."

The party was loud. The bass on the Bose system pumped out its beat. Emma walked in and bumped into numerous people just trying to get in the door. The living room was busy. The sofas had been pushed back, and the wooden floor, removed of its coffee table, had become the dance floor. LED lights hung from the ceiling and couples danced sensually to the beat of the sexy music.

Emma looked around to see who she knew. Wow, who didn't she know? The whole school seemed to be here. She took a moment to take it all in. Some girls were dressed like her: a combination of cute and sexy. A sundress, strapless, of course, and maybe just a little too short, platform shoes to help even out her height with Luke, a sultry smile, and some colorful makeup with matching jewelry. Others, on the other hand, looked like they came out of the bedroom. See-through shirts that looked more like lacey lingerie and tight short shorts. One girl was wearing black stockings and a man's black top hat.

Emma pretended she felt comfortable and moved behind Luke into the kitchen, which was buzzing with conversation. *The punch is probably spiked,* Emma thought. The cooler was open for a convenient grab, and the counter was full of goodies and, of course, pizza. Drew, a football player Luke knew, seemed to be the bartender for the evening. As Emma poured herself a glass of Coke, he threw in a shot of whiskey. "No thanks," Emma said, reaching for another cup.

"It doesn't taste any different. You'll like it," he promised. Emma started to say something but couldn't get the words out before he said, "It's senior year. You need to have at least one taste." The way he looked at her, she could tell he knew she was a virgin. *Alcohol* virgin she mentally corrected herself. Annoyed she walked away to find Luke.

Jordyn walked up and embraced Emma. "Hey, girl, yooou look awe … some." She was already slurring her words.

After looking at Jordyn, Emma suddenly remembered why she never drank. It was the first time she realized the choice was not because of her parents but because of her friends who made fools of themselves when they drank.

The party was good and no one crashed it, but Emma's mood was spoiled. Luke danced with her, talked with her and their friends, played football in the moonlight, but never once did he so much as kiss her. He wasn't unaffectionate, but it wasn't what Emma had in mind.

Kate wasn't able to settle down, and finally, the nurse had come in and insisted that Eliza leave. Kate had resisted at first, not letting go of Eliza and screaming at the nurse.

"It's okay. Kate, I won't leave. I'll be right outside. Call me if you need me. It'll be okay."

Later, the nurse had come out and told her that Kate had fallen asleep. That gave Eliza a little peace but not much. How could she handle this? She had no idea what to do. She wasn't studying psychology. She hadn't been close with a suicide survivor before. Yet here she was—all Kate had. Eliza wasn't used to having this kind of pressure. She had helped friends before in times of crisis, but could she help Kate?

Then other feelings started nagging at her. What happens after this? Sure, today she could be at the hospital, and tomorrow. Then she could visit, but she couldn't ignore her studies and responsibilities indefinitely. When would they release Kate? Would Kate become normal again, or would she need more than just a friend? She might need counseling or something. Eliza knew she couldn't fill that role. After they released Kate, would she be out of danger, or should she worry more about Kate and this happening again? How could she protect Kate from herself? Without that silly letter, Kate would have been dead.

She needed help. Bowing her head, she prayed again for herself and Kate.

The car ride home was an eerie, purposeful silence. Emma was in a terrible mood and Luke had no idea what to make of it. What had he done this time? Making sure there was nothing he could think of, he asked her, "What's wrong?" He braced himself for her response.

"I'm just upset."

She sat there silently and finally said, "Why didn't you touch me?"

Luke looked a little confused. "I did. I danced with you, held your hand, and even rubbed your back, remember?"

"No, I mean touch. Why didn't you kiss me or snuggle me or make out with me?"

"I kiss you all the time." Luke clearly wasn't getting it, so she may as well just be blunt.

"I thought you might have … you know, taken me upstairs. Maybe made love to me again?" Having said it out loud, Emma felt shy. Perhaps Luke, despite what he said, really did regret them being together.

Luke looked lost in thought. He actually looked a little angry. Luke had hardly ever been angry, but he looked it now. Then he seemed to calm down enough to turn and look at her. "That's what you wanted? I'm sorry to disappoint you. Emma, I didn't know, but even if I had, we wouldn't have made love. I'm not going to ruin your reputation in front of the whole school just to show off. Our love means more to me. What you see in there is trashy, Emma. People have sex because it's a fad, a cool thing, or because they are too drunk to know up from down. We have the real thing. If you want, we could go upstairs now." They had just pulled up in front of Emma's house.

Luke had spoken with passion and gentleness, but Emma was still hurt. Couldn't he understand she wanted the world to know they were together like that? She wanted to tell everyone else what she knew, that Luke was hers.

"No, my parents might wake up," she answered.

Luke smiled. "It's been a good night. They'll be other chances for us. How about a kiss?" Emma couldn't resist. Even though she was upset and didn't feel like having sex, she still craved him, wanted him. She laid her head on his shoulder. He cradled her in his arms and kissed her. Her whole body felt like it was on fire as he gently pulled back and said good night.

Chapter 10

Eliza peeked in at Kate. She was still zonked out. It was one o'clock in the morning, but Eliza couldn't leave. Much to the nurse's dismay, Eliza decided to spend the night. Kate's room had a comfy lounging chair—not the best for sleeping on, but at least she would be here if needed. In the meantime, she had updated her mother who had taken off work and was coming in tomorrow. Mr. Grant was also fully debriefed on the situation and gave Eliza the rest of the week off, which was more than generous. He said he would see what he could do about Kate's "situation," whatever that meant.

Eliza was at least glad her mom was driving up. She would be able to keep Eliza sane and deal with the doctor. She might even be used as a sort of impromptu guardian, even though Kate was already nineteen.

The Hope of Eliza

Poor girl. What had made her feel so depressed that she thought the only way out was death? Eliza was pretty sure it wasn't just the scholarship. Oh, that reminded her that she hadn't even asked if she had gotten the scholarship so that she could give it to Kate. She hadn't discussed it with Mom, but under the circumstances, if Kate was able to return, she wanted her to be taken care of financially. She was pretty sure Mom would also see it that way.

Sighing, Eliza stared at her friend. She was breathing deeply now. She curled up on the sofa and grabbed a blanket that the nurse had brought in. She didn't think she could sleep, but perhaps she had underestimated how exhausted she was.

However, the night wasn't peaceful for Eliza or Kate. Kate half-woke startled by some very real nightmares. Eliza would jerk up and ask what was wrong and then, along with the nurse's assistant, try to get her settled back down. After the last episode, Eliza turned away from Kate and the nurse's assistant, who was ever present on suicide watch, and just cried. Silent tears rolled down her face. She was afraid for Kate. How could someone recover from something like this?

All the talk was about Tyler's party. Well, most of it. Valentine's Day was right around the corner, and of course, every senior was counting down the days till their wild spring break trips. Emma wasn't sure if she'd be allowed to go on any of these trips, but the thought that she might made her crazy. She would go with Luke, of course. Maybe they could spend their time on the beach. Maybe they could do something big like visit New York. If she could convince her parents, this might be the best thing that happened to her senior year. Well, one of the best anyways.

Jordyn chatted about how the party went. It was lively, she said. She talked about the dancing, the beverages, and most importantly, who hooked up with who.

Emma was quick to join in. "How was Mason as a date?"

Jordyn stopped to think for a moment. "He was boring," she finally answered, "and a little strange."

"Why? What did he want you to do?" asked Sara.

"That's the thing. He danced, but he didn't, you know, put his hands on me, and he pushed me back when I tried to dance closely with him."

"So because he respected, you unlike some of your sex-driven maniac boyfriends, he was weird?" Sara laughed.

"It wasn't just that. He didn't drink. He was way too quiet. He was nice to talk to though. You know, he really seemed to listen. I guess he was okay. Just not my idea of fun."

"Did you ask him why he wouldn't do any of those things?" asked Emma.

"Yeah. He said he was into the whole God thing."

"Oh," the girls both said.

Jordyn quickly changed the subject. "Did you see Jenny at the party?"

"Yeah. What was she doing there? She never hangs with us." And by "us," Sara meant the popular elite of the school.

Jordyn continued. "She was there with Zachary Johnson!"

"*What?*" Both Emma and Sara leaned in.

"No, she wasn't," Emma stated.

"I'm telling you she was. That's how she got invited." Emma took a moment to absorb what Jordyn had said. Jordyn had never been wrong about these things before, but Zachary Johnson was the hottest guy in school, next to Luke, of course. Six feet tall and huge muscles was all the charm that boy needed. Emma had known Zachary since elementary school. He was famous for going out with the hottest girl and then the next hottest girl. Jenny was not hot! Lookwise, she was okay, but she didn't dress the part. She was both smart and practical, a no-high-heels-in-the-winter kind of girl. Plus Jenny hardly ever wore makeup. She just seemed way too plain for Zachary. How had she gotten his attention?

"When did this happen?" Sara asked.

"I heard that it's been in the works for about a month, and then, before the party, he officially asked her out."

"You can't be serious! They won't stay together. You know that, right?"

"How do you know, Emma?" Sara wanted to know more from a gossip standpoint than a caring one.

"Because ..." Emma's cheeks became red as they all stared at her, waiting for her answer. "Jenny is a virgin."

"That'll change," Jordyn remarked.

Emma shook her head. "I don't think so, Jordyn. Maybe he could trap someone else, but something tells me he doesn't care about that."

"How could he not?"

"Well, he didn't take care where his social reputation is concerned. He took her publicly to the biggest party. If he's willing to risk all that for her, perhaps she's special," Emma explained.

"Emma, you are too naïve. He's good-looking and smart. He knows she'll fall for him eventually. I wouldn't be surprised if she's already changing herself for him. She should start with fashion, if you know what I mean."

Emma thought Jordyn was being a little harsh. She couldn't see Jenny even going out with him if they didn't have some kind of agreement. After all, Jenny had turned down several guys. That was how she had earned her virgin reputation. Emma didn't see her giving that up for anybody, even Zachary. Jenny seemed like the kind of person who was always herself and didn't pretend for anyone. She had looked nice at the party, but nothing to indicate she had changed herself for him. Jordyn had this one figured out all wrong. Emma just knew it.

Eliza jolted awake. She hadn't thought she had fallen asleep, but apparently, she had at one point. Stretching, she sat up sleepily. Kate was staring at the TV but looked away as Emma woke. "Hey, Kate, do you want anything?"

Kate turned slowly toward her. "I don't really feel like anything right now."

"How about a good book or some decent food?"

"Thanks, but no. I think I need a little time."

"Do you want me to leave?"

"No. No, you don't have to."

"Okay …" Eliza was uncertain about what to say next so she turned her attention to the TV for a moment and then picked up her phone. There was one text from her mom that just said, "Almost there." Eliza decided to step out and call her mom.

"Hey, honey. How are you?"

"Fine … I think."

"Is Kate up?"

"Yeah, but I don't think she wants company."

"No problem. I'll be outside. Eliza, dear, have you had any breakfast?"

"No …"

"Great. I would like to take you out. That will give us time to talk. Do you think Kate will be okay?"

"Yeah, they have someone watching her. I'll let her know."

"Okay. I'm getting off the highway so I should be there in five minutes."

"Okay. I'll meet you downstairs."

Eliza stepped back into the room. "Are you sure you're not hungry? You really should eat."

"No, I'm fine."

"A book?"

"If you know of any happy ones."

"I think I have a few in mind."

A nurse stepped in. "Good morning, everyone. How are we doing?" Kate didn't answer the friendly nurse. The lady, whose name was Kristina, didn't appear put off but went around checking charts and documenting.

"The doctor will be in around ten to see you, dear." Surprisingly Kate didn't even ask about when she would be allowed to go home. After Nurse Kristina finished her routine checks and asked if Kate needed anything, she left, promising to be back with a light yogurt just in case Kate changed her mind.

Eliza sat on the side of her friend's bed. She took Kate's hand in hers and looked her in the eye. "I'm really glad you're going to be okay." She brushed back a few tears that had escaped. "We're going to make it through all of this, I promise." Kate embraced her, shedding a few tears of her own. Eliza pulled away, glancing at the time on her phone without letting go of Kate's hand. "I'll be back before the doctor comes in. I'm going to get some breakfast. Call me if you need anything. I won't be gone long."

Kate nodded and even attempted a smile. "I think I'll try to sleep."

Sleep didn't come for Kate though. She kept thinking about all the ones she loved. She felt herself lucky to be alive, kind of, but she still didn't know what she had to live for. Eliza had proven to be a real friend, but was that enough? Would their friendship last a lifetime like family would?

She let her thoughts drift to her sister and brother. What would they think if they knew she had tried to commit suicide? They would hate her; she was sure. Her sister might be too young to understand. She wanted them back. She wanted to fix the problems that had started with her parents, but she couldn't even take care of herself. Who would trust her enough even just to visit her siblings?

Angry tears slid down her cheeks. Tears that she thought she didn't have enough of, and then, there they were again. A constant companion to one as distressed as she was.

Chapter 11

Emma had rehearsed the beautiful evening she had planned in her mind. She wasn't sure why, but she desperately wanted Luke again. Feeling she couldn't wait, she asked her dad for some spending cash and booked them a hotel room for after dinner. Luke would be so surprised. They wouldn't spend the night, of course, but they could have a little fun. She had already checked in around two o' clock so that they wouldn't attract any suspicion coming in together. Now she waited for him to pick her up.

Luke drove his shiny red Camaro up to the large house. He got out in his black tux with matching black bowtie. He held a bouquet of roses in his hands. As soon as he saw her on the front porch, he lost his breath. His whole body longed for her. She was wearing a red low-cut dress that was perfect for a romantic Valentine's Day dinner. Her hair was pinned up, but loose curls floated down all around her face. She wore an eager smile. Oh, how he loved her. He planned to take her to the most expensive place in town, and if she was up for it, find a private spot somewhere afterwards.

Emma came over to him, kissing him sweetly. Her mom followed, holding the camera in one hand. "Don't you look handsome, Luke?" she beamed like she was his own mother. "Okay you two, stand by that tree over there. Oh, so cute!"

Mr. Steward pulled up in his Lamborghini. He waved to them as he eased into the garage.

"Honey," she called to him, "come take a picture with your lovely daughter."

Mr. Steward smiled. Still dressed in his business suit, he looked the part.

"Daddy!" Emma squealed, practically jumping up and down.

"May I?" he asked Luke, as if he was cutting in on the dance floor.

"Why, of course," Luke said, backing away just in time for her arms to fling around her daddy's neck. Luke knew this moment was special for Emma.

"Okay, I'd better let you go," he said, bending to kiss Emma. "It looks like your young man is waiting for you. Have fun, kids."

"We will, Daddy!"

Luke held the door open for her. "Bye, Mr. and Mrs. Steward."

"Bye." Emma waved.

Loraine had gotten the call yesterday afternoon. A concerned nurse at the hospital had somehow tracked her down. One of her babies had tried to commit suicide. Loraine didn't know why she called all her children "babies" or why she felt the pain of responsibility, even after they were no longer in her care, but something propelled her to care the way she did. So without a second thought, she let the office, where she still worked as a social worker, know she wouldn't be in for a few days, called her husband, and took the first flight to Iowa. Poor Kate.

When they were found, the responsible teenager had been providing her siblings with far more care than they were probably accustomed to from any adult in their lives. The mother hadn't reported the children missing for two weeks. Even after that, it had taken them almost a year to track down the kids. Those months with the police involved had been intense, and the whole community thought they were dead, but eventually, someone had noticed something and that was how she got assigned to Kate. Loraine still didn't know how she had been able to rent an apartment at sixteen, but that girl was unstoppable. Well, almost.

Kate was so angry; the children were being split up and torn away from her, literally torn out of her arms. That scene still burned in Loraine's mind to this day. Loraine couldn't do anything. Not many families wanted three kids, the oldest having turned seventeen by now. Unfortunately, the kids had been split up, but only the youngest had ended up in a good spot. Of course, she had moved three times prior to her current home. She had thought Kate was on the right track. Not many kids who aged out of the system had a plan, but Kate had been specific. What had changed?

Loraine's mind went back to that conversation she had had with Kate a few days before she started the internship. She hadn't known what to expect. A part of her hoped that she would be happy for her sister to have a good mom and dad. But she also knew that Kate had her heart set on adopting her. Even after years apart, she had remained a devoted sister. She remembered every birthday, took advantage of every opportunity to see them, and wrote letters to them or called them when she was allowed.

And then there was the call yesterday. Yes, her sister's adoption had been finalized and Robby had been sentenced to juvie for drug-related charges. Now Loraine was walking up to Kate's room, again unsure of her reaction. They had had a strained relationship because of decisions that were made about her siblings, but still she had always felt they had a connection. She loved each of her kids beyond what she could express. She wanted to make their lives better, but sometimes she felt her job involved more of watching them suffer than helping them. These kids had been dealt a bad hand, and even good families often couldn't get them through the emotional damage that had been dealt to them as early as one day old.

Tentatively, she pushed open the door. Kate had her back toward the door and didn't even bother to lift her head. She wasn't sleeping. Loraine approached the bed. "Kate," she whispered.

Emma was wowed by the restaurant. The elegant atmosphere, the expensive and tasteful menu, and the indoor water fountains that sectioned off the restaurant set the place apart from anywhere they had ever been. Luke had picked the perfect place. No one from school was here. How he managed to afford all this, she didn't know, but she didn't care. She felt like a princess. She was almost a little too anxious during dinner. She hoped Luke had the same thing on his mind.

It turned out he did. Leaning forward, he whispered, "Want to go somewhere tonight where we can be together?"

Emma responded, "I have a surprise for you."

They left as soon as Luke paid the bill. Emma insisted on driving so it would be a surprise. Although she wasn't as experienced with driving a stick, Luke had taught her fairly well, and they managed to get to the hotel without stalling. She made Luke close his eyes, blindfolded him, and walked in the back door. She led him to the bed and made him sit down. She pulled off his blindfold with gusto.

He just stared at her. "How did you?"

She put her finger to his lips to shush him. "I have another surprise," she said playfully. And boy did she ever.

My … did she look stunning. Luke still hadn't recovered before she started kissing him. He was lost in a trance and his instincts took over completely. Never had he imagined them having this much freedom. Kissing and holding her, they became one again.

And this time when it was over, he held her in his arms. He let out a sigh of contentment.

"Did you like my surprise?" she said in a sultry tone.

He only smiled.

It was so good to see Mom. Only problem was that Eliza felt tense leaving Kate at the hospital. Because of this, they popped into a small diner that assured them that they could get their food quickly. Eliza, for the first time remembering that she hadn't eaten in more than twenty-four hours, tried not to gulp down her food in one swallow.

Mom smiled amused, but she didn't say anything about her manners. "How are you, honey?"

"Oh, Mom, I'm glad you are here. I don't know what to do. I feel so lost and hopeless." Mom only nodded, encouraging Eliza that she was here to listen. "I can't believe this is happening. All because of money; it doesn't make any sense."

"Sometimes, there are things beyond what someone can see on the surface that can affect you deeper than anyone knew could be possible. It won't be possible perhaps for you to understand Kate's feelings completely, but you must try to find out what was happening in her heart. Gently though. She may not be ready for in-depth conversations about her decision, but you two have become close over the months. And my guess is you're all she has now. She may not want to talk, but encourage her. Show her you are trustworthy with her darkest secrets, her deepest pains. You must show her you don't feel anything different about her. Of course, the circumstances of your friendship are different, but Kate is the same person."

"I know, and I love her the same, but it's hard for me to treat her the same knowing what she had been through."

Mom reached across the table and squeezed her daughter's hand firmly. Her gaze held conviction. "You must look at Kate the person, not the choice she made." Then barely audibly, she commented, "Out of everyone, there were only two people who did that for me."

Eliza's gaze met her mother's sharply. "Who?" She saw her mother shift uncomfortably in her seat. Would she respond to the question this time?

"This isn't about me; it's about Kate."

"Mom, I have to know. Why don't you ever talk about your past? What happened to your parents?"

Mom's face clouded with a pain Eliza couldn't describe and almost couldn't bear to look at. For a moment, she thought she had gone too far and that her mom might just walk out and leave her at the diner.

A silent tear slid down her mother's face and she spoke with quiet dignity, making it apparent that the past still hurt her, yet she had somehow moved on. "Eliza, I ... I love you, baby. I don't want to spoil our lives with the past that still haunts me. I don't want to cause you the pain that I have suffered. I made my own choices. I don't want you to suffer from them more than you have to."

The Hope of Eliza

A dread came over Eliza. What was her mother talking about? She wanted to scream, "What happened?"

Her mother took a deep breath, regained control, and replied. "What you need to know is that you are looking at a woman who was abandoned by everyone she knew and loved and left alone to care for you. I never regret raising you alone. You are worth every pain I've ever been through. I just hope you haven't suffered without a father or grandfather. I could never give you the life I wanted to give you. I've always felt I don't have enough financially for what you really deserve. All I can think about is how I won't be able to help you through college, won't be able to pay for your wedding. You are such a deserving daughter, but my own choices have put us here."

"No, Mom. You've always been enough. I've never been lacking. I would never trade you for another person's family in a million years. For real. I've always felt blessed to have a mother as selfless and as loving as you. I really feel sorry for other girls who don't have what I have. Look at you. You're at the hospital to support me and someone you've never met. And look at Kate. No one, not even her mother, came. But you're here. You love her even though you haven't got the chance to meet her. You are the most amazing woman I have ever met. I hope I can be the mother you are to me to my kids someday." Eliza scooted beside her mother, embracing her. "I really mean it every word. Please don't be sad."

Eliza wiped a tear from her mother's face. Her mother was beautiful. Her blonde hair hung loosely about her shoulders. It was the natural blonde that everyone else tried to achieve by dying their hair. At thirty-six, her mother looked more like she was in her twenties. Her blue eyes glimmered and reflected the sunlight coming through the windows. Even as she cried, she looked like an angel.

Eliza squeezed her mom's arm. "I love you."

"I love you too. We should get back to the hospital so you don't miss the doctor." Her mom excused herself to the rest room.

Eliza felt warm inside. She never wanted her mother to be the way she was today—so vulnerable, so sad, feeling as if she wasn't good enough. Of course, any girl wants a daddy to love her, but she needed her mom to understand that she was more than enough. She had enjoyed comforting her mother. But she never wanted to see that look on her face again. She would do anything she could to make her mom as happy as she herself was. She had given her everything; everything she had done had come from her heart. She never complained about the burden of caring for a little girl on her own.

Eliza wanted to know what had happened to her grandparents, her dad, and her mother's friends, but she was more concerned with making her mother happy, even if that meant leaving the past in the past until she was ready to talk about it. She would wait patiently. Eliza might have always had a secret longing to meet her dad just once, but she would probably never do that. Whatever had happened between them was bad enough that her mom had never talked about her dad in a good or a bad way. They must have been in love if Mom still felt too much to mention him. Why had he left them? And more importantly, why had he never come back?

Chapter 12

Life went on like normal. Luke missed Emma in a way he couldn't explain, but he tried to hold back his desire. She was young and still so innocent. He wanted them to be together, but it would be a long time before he proposed and they married. They would have to be careful. No sense in hurting their families. College would be a different story, but right now, he wanted to be cautious. But it was hard, considering how much he wanted her.

Eliza's mom agreed to stay in the waiting room until the doctor left, to give Kate some privacy. Eliza dreaded what she might find behind that door but arrived as planned around 9:30. Eliza opened the door and saw a woman in her mid-thirties sitting in

The Hope of Eliza

a chair and leaning over Kate's bed, gently stroking her hair out of her face. She was whispering words of kindness to Kate. The moment Eliza saw the woman's eyes, she found them to be full of love. A love so deep and a heart so much in despair, Eliza thought this must surely be her long-lost mother. Maybe she had changed her mind after all. Maybe some things were getting settled between them.

Just as she was about to turn back to afford them some privacy, Kate called, "Eliza, come meet Loraine Greenfield."

Okay, not Mom, she thought, unless she had gotten remarried. "Hi, nice to meet you; I'm Eliza."

"Pleased to meet you. I've heard a lot about you these past few hours. I'm glad Kate has a friend like you."

Eliza gulped, trying to figure out the situation. Kate filled in the pieces. "She is, or was, my social worker."

Eliza's eyes widened with surprise. *Was Kate an orphan?* She remembered Kate referencing her mom a few times. Nothing positive, but Eliza had been under the impression that she was alive. *How had Kate been in foster care? And how come I never knew?* She thought painfully. Eliza considered Kate her best friend. Kate knew everything about her, but apparently, that didn't go both ways. Stuffing down the anger that began to rise, Eliza nodded. "We need to talk."

"Yeah, I bet you have a lot of questions," Kate said.

Eliza blushed. Here Kate was in the hospital on what could have been her deathbed, and Eliza was worried about who? Herself. It hurt to admit she was so selfish, but Eliza had also been through a lot these past twenty-four hours, and for the first time, she wondered if her emotions would hold. Perhaps this was a better conversation to have after a good night's sleep, if that would even be possible. "Don't worry about it now. We need to get you better and find out what we have to do to let you come home."

"Eliza, can I speak with you for a moment?" Loraine asked.

"Of course." They stepped into the hall, out of hearing range, and walked a short distance to the little chairs stationed along the wall. Loraine had dark hair and was professionally dressed, despite the fact that she wasn't at the office.

"I think, she's okay, Eliza. I know you're worried. She seems emotionally stable. Well, as stable as she can be. I've been with Kate since she was seventeen. I'm assuming you may not know much about her past. I want her to share that with you. She will, because you're the first person she has met that she can really trust. I'm happy to have you by her side because I can't stay. I'm up here for personal not job-related reasons. I needed to make sure this won't happen again. I think she regrets trying to take her life, which is encouraging because she probably won't attempt it again. However, she needs you more than ever now. I know how hard this is. It's an extreme situation, and I'm sure you have things of your own to deal with. However, I'm also certain if you take care of yourself, you two will continue to be good friends. I won't go into the details of her past because I think it needs to come from her, but here is what I will say: her life has been composed of mostly tragedy.

"She doesn't need your pity; she needs your hope, Eliza. I hear you are an optimist who is hungry to experience all the good things life has to offer. It's a miracle you are here with her and have chosen to stick by her. I am extremely grateful. This part of my life is hard when I can't help them."

"You're wrong. You have helped. I've never seen her look so peaceful and relaxed since before. I appreciate you coming up here."

The woman smiled. "I'm leaving her in your capable hands. Call me if you need any advice from a counseling standpoint. Don't get me wrong. I don't expect you to take on all this by yourself. I intend to have Kate work with a professional, but I know a huge part of her healing process depends on your continued friendship."

Eliza nodded. She took all the woman had to say to heart. It was scary. Would Kate relapse? This woman was certain she wouldn't, but Eliza wasn't sure. She didn't want things to go badly between them and something bad to happen.

"I have confidence in you. You seem like a strong woman, Eliza."

"Thanks."

"I'm going to go say good-bye to her and help in any way I can. Please contact me and keep me updated. I'm working on getting her help for her education and counseling needs. I feel confident these will be met by the state."

"That would be wonderful."

Emma stroked her long, blonde hair. It was damp with silent tears, tears for herself, tears for her broken heart. How she wished she could have a friend right now. Only she did, right? Lots of them, in fact. But then why was she alone? At the most desperate time in her life, she felt completely alone. The whole world seemed to be against her.

She reached for her cell phone, but the screen was blank. How she wished Luke would call her, or anyone would call her for that matter. Still, she sat in her dark room, helpless.

The Hope of Eliza

What would she do?

⁂

Eliza listened carefully to everything that the doctor was telling Kate. "The drugs you took could have done severe damage to your internal organs; however, we have been monitoring them and feel fairly confident that none of them have suffered significant damage. I attribute this to the fact that you were found right away before your body had time to fully process the drugs through your system. From a medical standpoint, you are fine. Your body has come off the drugs and is stabilized. But because of your circumstances, we are required to keep you here a minimum of twenty-four hours in which you will have a CNA, which is a nurse's assistant, with you at all times. You will be evaluated by a psychologist who will determine when you can leave. Do you have any questions?"

"Yeah. When can I get my stuff back? My clothes, my necklace, aren't here."

"It's standard protocol to keep these things until we are sure that you are no longer a danger to yourself. These items will be released to you when you check out of the hospital."

Kate just nodded wearily. She seemed to sink into despair. Eliza thought she was regretting how much this situation had truly cost her. Not only had it put strain on her friendships, it had taken away her freedom. She was almost a prisoner, being constantly watched and now evaluated. She had lost a lot of small privileges like wearing her own clothes. She was allowed only plastic silver wear, but without a plastic knife. To the hospital, these were precautions, but to Kate, it must feel like she had thrown away her basic rights when she decided she was going to take her own life. Eliza was relieved that although they were monitoring visitors closely, so far, no one had been turned away.

Eliza was also very relieved that no terminal effects from the medication she took would be causing her any future problems. It would be interesting to hear what the psychologist would have to say.

Chapter 13

Emma strode into the locker room. Her friends were excited for the big basketball game. But she wasn't feeling it. She felt sick. She could just imagine Luke. He'd be all pumped up, ready to cream their rival. His white skin, awesome, out-of-place, sweaty hair, and bulging, glistening muscles combined with that competiveness would make him easy to look at. Only Emma didn't want to look. She hadn't been ashamed of what they had done. At least she had tried to convince herself of that. But it was different now. Now she knew the truth. She knew the consequence of their passion. She was pretty positive. Emma was never late, not even a day. She had tried not to panic when she hadn't started. Being on birth control for cramping should have ensured this wouldn't happen. What did the box say? The pill was 99.9 percent effective. Could she really be the .1 percent?

She hadn't believed it. In denial after two days, she had gone to Wal-Mart. She had bought a shirt to cover it up and gone through the self-checkout line just to be sure. Being in that aisle had been embarrassing enough, especially when an old woman had walked past her. She swore the woman had figured out what she was shopping for. Emma hadn't stayed to find out. She left with the first brand she recognized.

Agonizingly, she had taken the pregnancy test and then stared at it. Those three minutes of waiting could have killed her.

When that little line popped up, she dropped it out of shock. Now the shock had worn off, slightly. She knew the truth.

She was pregnant!

She realized that she had wanted Luke to call in that moment because she wouldn't have been able to hide the truth. Now, she realized she didn't want to tell him. Why? Was she afraid of his reaction? All she needed was to feel his strong arms around her, but somehow, she knew that wasn't going to be his reaction. In every movie she had seen, the first line out of the boy's mouth was "Are you sure?" Oh, she was sure all right. It had now been a week since she should have started, and three pregnancy tests later, her fears were confirmed.

She couldn't face him. Not even on the court. The last week, she had been avoiding his gaze. He kept telling her he felt bad. Emma had denied that their having sex again was why her mood had changed. She had assured him she wasn't feeling bad about it. Though they had kissed, they hadn't gone that far again. Now Emma knew no matter what they did, it couldn't get any worse.

What was she going to do? How could she tell him? "Hey, babe, I'm glad you want to be with me forever because guess what. We're going to have a baby"

"We're pregnant" or maybe she should try "Guess what else happened when you made love to me?

"You know how I said it was fine because I was on the pill? Well ..."

Every turn seemed wrong.

"Emma, come on, girl. We've got to go," said one of the girls.

Smiling, Emma went out the door. Maybe the distraction of the game would be good for her. Her excitement began to build as she heard the fans cheering. The team had just broken the huddle. Luke ran onto the court, locking eyes with Emma for a split second before the game started.

That moment had been enough to tear Emma's heart out. All the trust he had in them, all the hopes for their future, his eager youth longing for success all added up to one thing: a destroyed dream. She was about to destroy him. Though it wasn't her fault, she felt every bit of the guilt. If she wasn't ashamed before, she certainly would be now. Her life, her friends, her family—all those reputations ruined in a moment of sweetness. They were in love. It was okay.

Why didn't it seem that way now?

※

Eliza figured it was about time she called Mr. Grant, again. She updated him on the situation, figuring honesty with some discretion would be the best way to keep Kate in the internship. After updating him on the whole situation and the report from the doctor, which said that Kate would be able to leave the hospital in a few days if the psychologist cleared her, Mr. Grant informed her that she had won one of the scholarships. Eliza, having already discussed it with her mother, told him that she would rather it go to Kate.

Mr. Grant listened and then said, "Don't worry about her. I will take care of Kate. Congratulations, Eliza. You really deserve this scholarship."

Eliza didn't know what to say. She would make sure Kate was going to stay on, but it seemed that Mr. Grant had already figured out another way. Did he take away someone else's scholarship and give it to Kate? Or did he pay for Kate himself? Hmmm ... Interesting ... She would just have to see how this played out. One thing was for sure: if Eliza had anything to say about it, Kate would continue on as an intern no matter what.

***

The afternoon passed slowly for Eliza. She had introduced Kate and Lorraine to her mother and they had all chatted about very routine and meaningless things. Then Loraine said her good-byes.

Kate dozed off and on. Eliza figured it must have something to do with the medication or mental exhaustion. She thought about what Loraine had said and wished she knew how to help Kate. Kate opened her eyes and Eliza offered to see about getting her some food. This time, Kate actually agreed. Eliza, eager for an excuse to leave the terrible room, went to find a nurse instead of just pushing the buzzer. And then she decided, after hearing all of Kate's options, that the cafeteria might be the best choice.

When she returned, she was shocked to find Danny kneeling at Kate's bedside. Apparently, keeping a suicide story at bay was harder than Eliza thought. His face was serious and held a tender expression. His hand clasped Kate's. Eliza tried to ignore the pang of jealousy that surged through her at that moment. Why was she jealous? She had no clue, but she couldn't stop her heart from beating faster. Eliza looked on for a minute observing

Danny's thumb running back and forth over Kate's pale hand. Wow. Word about Kate had gotten out faster than she thought it would.

Danny's voice interrupted her thoughts as if he were answering her unspoken question. "Of course, I was worried about you two. I wouldn't stop pestering Mr. Grant, until I got the truth. I don't think he has told anyone else yet," he was telling Kate. He embraced Kate lovingly, wrapping her in his strong arms. He kissed her on her head and said, "Don't worry. You'll get past all of this. Liza and I will help. We'll always be there."

He turned around, suddenly realizing that Eliza had entered the room. Eliza's mom watched all their expressions with sudden interest and a hint of amusement. "Eliza!" At first, his voice held a sweet concerned note, but then it soon took another turn completely. "Why didn't you call me?"

Eliza glanced around the room. She couldn't handle his question now. Suddenly, with him standing in front of her, it seemed ridiculous she never made the call, but in the moment, no choice had seemed right. Now she realized what she had put her friend through. She wanted to burst into tears. *Hold it together,* she told herself. But when she realized she couldn't, she started toward the door and rushed off to find the woman's bathroom. She had half-expected her mother to follow her, but nobody did. At first, she hid in the stall—tears overflowing. Funny thing was she had no idea why she was crying. All she knew was she was emotionally and physically exhausted.

After her fifteen-minute episode, she strode to the mirror to apply damage control. Only, all she had was water. Finally realizing all was hopeless, she pulled herself together. Walking out of the restroom, she was met by Danny. "Ahh, Danny, you scared me."

"Sorry."

"Have you been waiting all this time?"

Danny only nodded. "I figured you needed some space." Eliza nodded curious why he had come after her.

"I'm sorry, I was harsh, Eliza, but you have to understand how I felt knowing Kate was in a hospital—could have died—and you completely alone. Yet you didn't call me. I consider you guys my best friends since moving away from home. It hurts that you couldn't trust me with this."

Eliza didn't know what to say. His words, though kind and true, hurt so much. Feeling self-conscious but unable to control it, she burst into tears. In-between her tears, she managed to say, "I'm so sorry. I do trust you. I … I just didn't know what to do everything happened so fast. Besides, I didn't know if it was my place … you know?"

Danny felt his heart expand and leaned in to comfort her. "Ssshhhh, it's fine."

But Eliza wouldn't let herself off the hook that easily. "No, it wasn't right of me."

"Maybe not," he conceded, "but you did the best you could, given the circumstance."

Eliza didn't know why, but as she moved to hug her friend, she realized something between them had changed. Danny had always been a good guy, but for the first time, that wasn't enough. She wanted him to be her guy. Even though she suspected he might have feelings for Kate, she allowed him to hold her, to calm her, to protect her. When they returned to the hospital room, Eliza felt better. She felt more confident that things would be okay.

But when Danny offered to stay with Kate so that she could rest, she refused. She told him she couldn't leave Kate, which was only part of the truth. The truth was she wanted them all to be together. She didn't want to leave lonely and scared. She wanted to spend every moment she could with Danny. A part of her knew that she also didn't want to leave the two of them alone, either. This was a disaster.

What a perfect time to be falling for someone. The intensity of the last few hours seemed to have accelerated every emotion she had ever had about Danny. She felt more emotionally connected than before. Was this a real emotion, or could the circumstances alone be causing her to have these more than friendly feelings toward Danny?

Somehow, Emma had survived the intense game. Luke was everywhere. The game was so close that he had nearly played the entire time. He was focused, intense, and intimidating. However, all Emma noticed was that she couldn't look at him without feeling like she had betrayed him. She hadn't lied. She hadn't kept it from him. It had only been a week since she had first suspected, and she had to be sure before she was going to tell him.

Her best friend was playing three feet in front of her. The one she always felt safe with was right there! For once, he didn't feel like enough. Even if he didn't react badly, and he took her in her arms and said it would be okay, Emma knew he couldn't help her. Nobody could. Perhaps this was why some people believed in God. When problems became insurmountable, was it natural to believe there had to be someone who could fix it?

If so, was it natural to think that if the problem was big enough, and even the closest person to you couldn't fix it, then maybe God could, if He existed? Emma was starting to lose her mind. She had never believed in God. Her mother had said often enough,

"God can't exist. Look at the cruel world we live in. Either He doesn't exist or He is such a merciless, cruel being that no one would want to be associated with Him."

Sighing, Emma decided she would tell Luke tonight.

She walked out of the locker room only to find Luke waiting for her. That was unusual, as he always took longer to get ready after a game.

"Hey, sweetheart. Are you okay? You were in there for a while? Everyone is waiting for us to celebrate at John's Pizzeria."

Emma smiled. "I don't really feel like going. Could you drop me off on the way?"

His smile faded. "What's wrong? Are you sick?"

"I don't think so."

"All right, I'll bring you home."

Now Emma felt guilty. He had just scored the winning basket, and she hadn't even congratulated him. On top of that, he would be late to the party because he had to drop her off. "It's okay. I'll have Mom pick me up. You go."

He looked at her, hesitating. "Baby, I know you don't feel up to it, but can't you come? We don't have to stay for a long time. We'll just pop in. I really want you to go with me."

Emma couldn't disappoint him. "Okay, that sounds fine."

"Are you sure?"

"Yep. Maybe afterwards we can talk."

"About what?" he asked hesitantly.

"It's fine," she said, realizing that it was a lie she hadn't intended on telling. She had only meant to reassure him. She saw by his hesitation she would have to keep her tone upbeat if he was going to be able to relax with their friends. "Let's go." She kissed him on the cheek.

Chapter 14

At last, good news! After Kate's psych evaluation, which was done in private, they agreed to release her the following day. That would mean they would have the weekend before going back in to work. The psychologists seemed to have more answers to Eliza's questions than the doctor. When would she be released? What should her care look like once she was released? How could she help? What did Kate's mental health look like? All of these questions the psychologist was able to answer one-on-one with Eliza. Kate would be enrolled in professional counseling. She shouldn't spend time alone. She was confident of Kate's mental state but warned that it might be a long way to emotional recovery.

The Hope of Eliza

The next day, as promised, Kate was released. The psychologist explained what would be required on Kate's part to be healed. She would have to allow herself to be helped by friends and family. She would be moving in with Eliza. She would need to be honest with the counselor and with herself. She might want to keep a private journal to voice thoughts she was afraid to say out loud. She shouldn't isolate herself or allow herself to feel inferior.

She gave a few minor suggestions to Eliza and then they all left the hospital. Danny drove them all to the dorms, while Mom followed in Eliza's car. The three of them were going to help Kate move into Eliza's room. Mom would stay the night but would be off the following morning to make it back to work before Monday. She promised to be in touch with both Kate and Eliza.

———

The party was actually fun. The guys recounted every success play-by-play and magnified every one of their and each other's accomplishments. If Emma hadn't been to the game, she was certain she wouldn't have missed very much because the guys seemed to replay it second by second. She beamed when they started teasing her about Luke's impressive shots and how maybe it was all because his lucky charm was there cheering for him.

"I wasn't cheering for him. I was cheering for the whole team," she explained.

"Ha," said Tommy, "but if it were up to you, the cheer's lyrics would change from 'Go, go Lions. Let your roar out ... Don't hold back now ... Show them *our* pride!' to 'Go, go Luke. get your game on ... Don't hold back now ... Just kiss me.'"

"It would not!" Emma shouted, her face turning bright red. She playfully slapped Tommy on the arm.

"Oww! That hurt. Hey, Luke, don't make her mad, okay?" he said mocking her.

Luke rose to her defense playfully. "Get out of here, Tommy. You're telling me that you can be fouled up and down the court, but you can't take a girl's slap. Hey, Emma, you should tell him if you wanted our cheers changed, you could."

"I don't want them changed," Emma defended. Luke just looked at her and laughed.

"What's so funny, you goofhead?" she shouted at him.

He howled louder. Her best friends were a great distraction, but when Luke asked if she was ready to leave, it all came back full force. She didn't want to tell him.

"Baby, I am so happy tonight. I don't think anything could ruin this day for me," Luke said. He had the world's most dazzling smile.

Emma smiled back. It would be a good time to tell him then. But listening as he elaborated, she knew she couldn't crush him. Especially now that he turned to a different topic. "Emma, you know the only thing that would make this day better? You. Do you want me, Emma Steward?"

When she hesitated, he quickly added, "We don't have to, if you're not ready ..." His voice trailed off.

"No," Emma stated. The fact was before this pregnancy, her body hungered for him. It hadn't stopped. She wanted him all right. "I want you, baby."

He wrapped his hand around hers and gently squeezed it. "I love you, Emma. I want you to be Mrs. Howard someday."

Emma couldn't help but smile. Maybe she had nothing to worry about where Luke was concerned.

After their dream night had ended, Luke dropped her off, giving her a final kiss. "I love you, baby. See you in the morning. I'm sorry we stayed out so late."

"I'm not," she said as she smiled saucily.

"I know you wanted to go home. I promised we'd go home soon."

"It's all right. I thought I wasn't in the mood, but it turns out this night was just what I needed." And she meant it.

At least, she thought so at the time, until she reached her bedroom. She cuddled up with the stuffed animal he had given her and wept. She cried until her lungs burned and hungered for oxygen. She cried until no more tears came out. Worse yet, she didn't even know why she was crying. Maybe it was true about pregnant women being so emotional, or maybe it was deeper. Because she didn't tell Luke, she felt guilty. A guilt she had never known before. She was sleeping with the man while feeding him and herself lies that everything was all right and that everything was normal.

She couldn't sleep. At 3 a.m., she finally gave up and took a shower. After that, her eyes weren't quite as puffy and her voice wasn't betrayed by sobs, but she still felt burdened.

Even if it wasn't fair, Emma needed Luke. Before she could change her mind, she dialed him up.

On Sunday, Eliza found herself rested and in better spirits. The weekend had passed smoothly. Kate was grateful to be out of the hospital and had decided to stay on and finish out the internship. She had received good news from Loraine, who got everything all set up for Kate's entire education (even the internship) to be paid by the state, meaning she didn't even need the scholarship. Apparently, since she was a foster child, the government would pay for her college. All along, she needn't have worried for her school expenses.

Loraine had filled out all the paperwork so that next week, when they started classes, Kate would be all set except for signing those papers herself. That took off a lot of pressure, but Kate was nervous to go to the office on Monday morning. Seeing everybody might be hard. Eliza tried to assure her that she would be fine and that everybody would be relieved, but even she was nervous about how everyone would respond, except for Danny, of course.

Eliza moved onto the bed, sitting cross-legged and looking at Kate. Kate smiled but didn't say anything. Eliza had been dying for Kate to be out with the truth, to help her to understand why she would do something like this. However, thus far, Kate had been in a world of her own. The only one who seemed to be able to draw her out of that world, for moments of time, was Danny. Eliza had accepted that as much as she was beginning to like Danny, she would hang back for Kate's sake. Kate needed Danny. Eliza had a feeling that Danny liked being needed.

She glanced at Kate again. "Are you waiting for a story?" Kate said with just a hint of irritation in her voice.

"We're friends. Your friendship means a lot to me. I've shared some very private information with you. I thought we knew each other well, but there is a whole side of you I never knew and that hurts. To be honest, I keep asking myself why you did it."

Kate sighed. She wished she didn't need to explain. Wished she could or that she didn't have to. She decided to tell Eliza the full story of her childhood and how she had ended up in this desperate situation. She started by asking her, "Has your heart ever just hurt so much you thought it might kill you? Has your heart ever been filled with so much grief you thought if you applied a little more pressure that the blood would escape killing you in an instant?"

Eliza looked more than sympathetic but said nothing. She waited as Kate launched into her story.

"I thought, there was no other way for me," she admitted at the end of her story.

Eliza, with tears in her eyes, looked Kate in the eye and just said, "You'll find another way." Kate was curious what she meant, but Eliza didn't elaborate other than to say she had found something that made her want to live even in the hardest times of her life. When Kate asked her what she meant, she replied, "Jesus is more than just going to church for me. He has been my best friend for a long time. He is the only person who understands me completely, loves me so much more than I can imagine, and always has the wisdom I need."

"How can he be your best friend? Like he talks to you?"

"Yes. Not audibly but through my thoughts."

Kate listened quietly trying to take it all in. She had known that Eliza was a Christian, but always knew there was something different about her than a lot of other "Christians" she had met. She wasn't quick to judge and was always quick to love and show compassion. Eliza had once said that's how all Christians were supposed to be because that's how Christ was. Kate learned from Eliza that *Christian* literally meant "little Christ." Yet Eliza was maybe the first person she had ever met who acted like the kind and compassionate Christ in the Bible.

What Eliza said intrigued but also confused Kate. Why would such a great God want to be best friends with people? How was it possible? Kate might have laughed it off, but the way Eliza talked about Him, with such passion and conviction in her voice, made her think seriously about all she had to say. Danny had also talked about Jesus in similar ways.

Luke bolted upright in his bed. His phone was ringing. "Dang it! It's three in the morning!" He fumbled for his phone. The screen showed, "Emma." "What the heck? She never calls me this late."

"Emma! What's wrong?" he asked fearfully.

"Nothing, baby."

"Then, why are you calling me at 3 a.m.? Can't this wait until morning?"

"No. Sorry, it can't. I can't keep it from you one more minute," she paused, her breath echoing in the phone.

Luke sighed. He knew this was coming. She had always been the good girl. She had never been with anyone before. Now, she felt guilty because they had had sex, again. She had started acting a little strange this last week. It was probably because of Valentine's Day, but that had been her idea. No, he corrected himself, *their* idea. He felt guilty for making her feel bad. He should have resisted a little longer, till … till he didn't know. Until she felt comfortable. But she had seemed comfortable. More than comfortable she had seemed eager.

"Baby, you can tell me."

She sobbed and took a breath. "I'm pregnant."

The news hit Luke like a big rig had slammed into the side of his head. "No, no honey, you're not."

"Yes," she said, almost angrily. "I should know. If you want proof, I'll take the test for you again."

This couldn't be happening. "Emma, it's impossible. You said so yourself. The birth control…"

"Well, it's true, birth control or not."

"Emma …" His silence rang through her ears.

She was so selfish for having called him and not telling him in person. She felt guilty as he fumbled for something to say. In a desperate voice, she called out, "Luke, what are we going to do?"

"Did you tell anyone else?"

"Of course not." Her voice sounded a little defensive.

"Don't worry. We'll figure it out."

After several minutes of silence, Emma mumbled in a teary voice, "I'm sorry, Luke. Are you angry with me?"

"No, baby," he said sympathetically.

Luke spent the next hour trying to calm her down. If he came over now, her parents would know something was up and that was the last thing they needed. He reassured her that he'd pick her up tomorrow. He needed to get off the phone so that he could think.

Chapter 15

Kate hadn't wanted to face the office so soon, but Eliza had insisted that they go together. Kate planned to say hi, not answer too many questions, and then excuse herself and go work in the dorms. She needed to be busy. Eliza had promised to work with her in the dorms so that she didn't have to be completely alone.

Eliza glanced at Kate's shocked face. Her reception was more like a hero coming back from war than a shameful "almost death." The room was decorated with balloons and streamers. A big welcome-back banner took up the entire back window and was signed by everyone. Kate's desk was stacked with brand-new school supplies. A pink and black backpack hung over her office chair. People had brought cake, ice cream, and sparkling apple cider, except for Stephanie and Jim, who had real champagne. Eliza couldn't believe it.

The best part was yet to come. Mr. Grant asked for everyone's attention. "Okay, everyone calm down. Kate, we are so glad to have you back. On behalf of your fellow interns, we would like to present you with this humble scholarship fund."

Kate took the card with shaky hands. She couldn't describe what had come over her. She was embarrassed, thankful, and quite frankly shocked. This handful of people she had just met formed an almost family. They all pulled together from their personal resources to help with her scholarship. They had all signed the card, which held a few thousand dollars in cash. Kate covered her mouth and stifled a sob. She was crying as she took turns hugging each one. When she got to Josh, she hesitated ever so slightly. Josh reacted before she could, embracing her and kissing her cheek. Eliza didn't know if anyone else noticed the single tear that stuck in the corner of his eye. He rubbed his hand up and down her back and refused to let go of her. If she didn't know any better, she would have said it was a very romantic, protective, reassuring hug. Kate didn't pull back either. Something had definitely changed. Eliza prayed that that change was Josh's heart. The majority of the funds came from Josh's family and from Josh himself, but no one knew that except Eliza and Mr. Grant.

Emma huddled on the couch in her living room. Her hair, tumbling over her shoulders, was tangled and unkempt. Had she cried here all night? He sat next to her. "Where are your parents?"

"They're out."

Luke didn't know where to start. He had rehearsed his thoughts so many times, but now, seeing her like this—this devastated—he didn't know if he could say what he needed to.

"Oh, Luke," she cried, reaching for him. "What are we going to do?"

Luke took a deep breath and said, "We have to abort it."

Emma was shocked. That definitely wasn't what she expected to hear. Did she hear him correctly?

"Emma, don't look at me like that. I feel the same way; I don't want to, but we both know this is the only solution. We can't give up our dreams, Emma. Both of us. We'd be ruined, and so would our reputations. Think about your family. We can't do this to them. You think your parents will accept you destroying their perfect world like this? Emma, we both know the consequences."

The Hope of Eliza

Luke took a deep breath. Once his feelings started, he couldn't stop the words from tumbling out. "Your mom can be … They'll probably kick you out or even disown you. You know that is a strong possibility. Tell me, Emma, am I wrong?" Emma melted into tears, realizing the truth in his words. Luke put his arm protectively around her. "Shhhh … It's all right."

At first, she had been mortified that he had suggested it, but as he kept talking, it started to make sense. Her parents had never even threatened to kick her out, but they didn't tolerate imperfections well. She knew they might do as Luke had said.

"I know that's our only option, but it's a part of us," she said, finally.

"Emma, we'll have children together in our future at the right time. This isn't our baby. It is an accident. It wasn't supposed to happen. Emma, it's not fair to us, and think of what kind of life it would have.

"They will kick you out, Emma. We went too far and they'll have to salvage some of their reputation. Then who would care for you and it? I would try, sweetheart. I'd get a tiny minimum-wage job and we'd move into a crappy apartment on the rough side of town that we couldn't afford. We'd be hungry and stressed. No one would help us. We'd start fighting, telling each other all the dreams we sacrificed for each other. I can't give you the life you have or the one you want. You've never known anything but this well-off and comfortable lifestyle. In no time, you'd be sick of our crappy home, our crappy car, and Top Ramen for dinner. You'd hate our life, and then you'd hate me."

"No!" Emma cried out.

He held his hands on her shoulders and forced her to look at him. "Yes, not today, not tomorrow, but some day when you have no friends left, you don't speak with your parents, you have no college degree, and no hope of anything better, you'll have to blame someone. What kind of life is that for us or our children? No child of mine is ever going to experience that, Emma. Do you hear me?"

He held her as she cried for almost an hour and finally left her asleep on the couch. Bending, he kissed her softly. "I love you, Emma."

And he thought he really did.

Kate stared at the envelope of money in her hand. Everyone had insisted she keep it, even after she had told them it was all taken care of. The tiny envelope held her dreams in it. The first thing she did with the money was buy a nice present for each of her siblings. For Robby, she had bought some books so

The Hope of Eliza

that he had something productive to do with his time. He also loved to draw, so she purchased a few sketchpads and sent them to him. For Carolyn, she had bought the American Girl Doll that she had always dreamed of owning.

After receiving the gift, Carolyn's new family purchased her dream pony to go with it. They had been wonderful surprises, but now she wondered what to do with the rest of it. Thanks to her recent experience with the system, she knew that her siblings could also go to college. She also knew that once she graduated the internship, she hoped to land a part-time job while continuing her own education. She was fine for now. She had thought to just put the money in savings, but the fact that she only had two years to be able to convince Robby that he needed to live with her meant that they would need a place of their own. A part-time job might not do it all, but she would at least have two years of school behind her.

She needed the money to work for her. After discussing her options with the bank, she decided she would invest the money for two years. Hopefully, this four thousand dollars would grow into something that would give her and Robby a chance at life. She intended to finish school and then move them both closer to Carolyn. She had never thought it possible, but it certainly looked like the Petersons could become their family. They had officially adopted Carolyn but took it upon themselves to visit Robby and invite Kate over. They had hinted that she may be welcome to stay the summer with them.

Maybe once they got to know her and Robby, they would trust them more with Carolyn. Already, they let her talk with them and visit Robby in juvenile detention, which Kate thought was impressive because of how young and impressionable Carolyn was, but the Petersons believed this was part of Carolyn's healing to be reunited with her family. It touched Kate. This was truly a miracle because Kate had never heard of anything like it happening. Could they really all stay together throughout the years, like she had planned?

Sure, her plans hadn't included prison or adoption, but they were together—not physically, but they wouldn't be separated. Their bond was somehow stronger than it was before. They were family.

Deciding to invest the money for their futures seemed like a good idea. She had no idea what their futures would look like, but she was quite certain they would need this generosity along the way.

Procrastinating wasn't helping her. Emma was becoming more depressed by the day. She couldn't hide the pregnancy very much longer. Though she hadn't gained a lot of weight, she wasn't herself. She tried to hide her tears in the restroom at school, at home in her room, and in the safe haven of her car. She couldn't keep doing this to herself; she had to do something. At least she wasn't sick. That would be a dead giveaway. It had only been a month since she had found out, yet her life had fallen apart. She couldn't blame all her emotions on the pregnancy. It was everything: the weight gain, the problems she was having with Luke, her own crazy roller coaster of emotions, and the fact that she couldn't stand to be around her friends anymore.

They talked about the usual stuff: their hairstyles, the boy that was driving them nuts, the new girl they couldn't stand, prom coming up, and many other useless topics. Sure, she would have joined the conversation a month ago, but now these things were of such little concern to her. The things that mattered to her would definitely be the talk of the school, if she told them. The problem was that it would be perceived as some fantastic joke. Her life would be the main event again, but not in the way she wanted it to be. She wanted ... She wanted ...

Heck, she didn't know what she wanted. She wanted someone to care about her, a friend who would want to listen to her, to try to understand how she felt. Of course, she didn't want to keep it.

She had no intention of keeping it, but surely Luke should understand she couldn't make a decision immediately. He argued, saying that the longer she waited, the harder it was going to be. She just needed some space, a little time, to sort out this jumbled mess. She didn't know what to think or how to feel. All she knew was that the only word to describe her condition was miserable.

Office life seemed to return to normal. School really packed the interns' schedules and took most of their time. It was a constant balancing act between school and work, but for Kate, the distraction was a welcome one. She seemed happier. The Petersons were more than happy to have Kate in the picture.

In fact, one week after a very long and wonderful phone conversation with Carolyn, Kate received pictures in the mail. They were Carolyn's school pictures. They were absolutely adorable. Carolyn was dressed in a fancy dress with matching little-girl high-heel shoes. She was smiling brightly, her hair dangling in a long braid with a pretty flower in it. Kate wasted no time hanging up the photos around the room.

Kate seemed to be in better spirits. Her brother, hearing about what happened, shifted out of a selfish fog and was calling Kate weekly. It seemed to Eliza that he was the same little boy who had tried to protect Kate all those years ago. Kate was good for him too. She called out the good in him and told him to avoid the company he'd been keeping. Prison, despite its negative effects, had a positive effect too. The dealers didn't want to contact Robby while he was inside those walls. She seemed relieved to hear that he was doing okay.

Eliza thought something else excited her as well. In two years, her brother would age out of the system. Kate hoped that they could be reunited at that point. She vowed to make something of herself in that time. His prison sentence was relatively light considering the circumstances, and with good behavior, he could be out before his eighteenth birthday.

Kate walked into the office that was fast becoming her home. All her friends were there. The only thing that bothered her was Josh. Things between her and Josh had been so weird lately that Kate tried to avoid him at all costs. Her heart was too fragile to convince herself there might be a chance that Josh was actually changing, though that is how it seemed. He started focusing on his work and dropped all the girl nonsense, even the flirting. He was somehow calmer. The way he looked at her disarmed her. He didn't look at her with pity like some people did. He didn't look like he was putting on a good face. He simply looked like he fully understood her. Granted, he had known her the longest. She honestly hadn't been able to predict everyone else's response either, but she definitely didn't expect this.

The change in Josh was radical. She started seeing more of the old Josh, the Josh she had known most of her life. Yet how was that possible? How could someone change overnight? Even if he had truly changed, she couldn't just act like he never hurt her. Her heart was being tempted to let him in again. Just this morning, she remembered the slight brushing of their hands as they both reached for the creamer. The smile he shot her was still etched in her memory. And what was with that hug he had given her when she came home from the hospital? Josh had acted like his long-lost love had come back from the dead. Before, she didn't seem to exist; now, it seemed she was the only one who existed in Josh's world. The way he had held her made her feel secure. She hadn't felt that way since ... Well, she never had. Even when she dated Josh before, the drama at home had kept her from ever really feeling safe. Now away from her parents, her siblings no longer her responsibility, a safe work environment and a moment in his arms had changed everything. Although she could sense Josh waiting for his moment to ask her for a second chance, she avoided him. She wouldn't let this happen again. Not after, all she had been through. Fall for him once: stupid. Fall again: she should be committed to a real psych ward.

Chapter 16

"Hey, Emma, wait up!" Emma slowed, rolling her eyes. Jordyn practically had to chase her down. "Hey, where have you been lately?"

"What do you mean I haven't missed school in months?" Emma stated matter-of-factly to her girlfriends who had her completely cornered.

"No, I mean you haven't been around."

Emma rolled her eyes. "Yes, I have." She tried to play it cool, but apparently Jordyn couldn't be put off that easily.

"Emma, don't play dumb. You haven't been around. You've been going off campus for lunch but never with us. You don't go to our locker, which means you are keeping all your books with you, which everyone knows is ridiculous. The only conclusion I can make is that you are avoiding us.

Why, Emma? Are we not cool anymore? Or is it because you and Luke aren't getting along?"

"What are you talking about? Luke and I are fine," Emma snapped.

"Emma, don't lie to me. I'm your best friend. The whole school knows that something's up with you two."

"Stop, Jordyn. I don't need this right now. I'm not in the mood for a lecture, and I don't care about what everyone thinks is going on between me and Luke."

"You say you don't care, but I know it's not true. Jimmy asked me to the prom. Did Luke ask you?"

"Not officially, but of course, we are going together," Emma stated rather defensively.

"Sorrrrry, Emma. I'm just concerned. That's all. Don't mind me." And with that she stormed off.

Emma bit her lower lip to stop the tears. Jordyn was right. She had been ignoring her friends, and Luke wasn't himself. Only she knew why her life had suddenly changed. A thought flittered across her mind. "Was Luke going to ask her?" Of course, he would, but why hadn't he asked her yet? Maybe he was waiting till after spring break. After all, it was right around the corner. Sniffling, she started down the hall toward her class with a new resolve.

Later, she saw Luke walking toward her in the hall.

"Emma." His face looked torn between wanting to show compassion and wanting to turn away from her completely. As if compassion won, he suddenly took her in his arms, where she melted down completely.

Sobbing, she choked, "Do you still love me?"

"Emma, don't ever ask that again. Of course, I love you. Look at me. I couldn't love you more. It's just that you're making this hard on us. Look, we can't go through with this. You know that as well as I do, but your indecisiveness is making us both stressed. But I love you. I always will, baby. I promise." She relaxed a little against his chest. "Once we get this taken care of, we'll be at the top of the world again. Just like before, love."

She tried for a brave smile she didn't feel and nodded. Sitting in her class and reflecting on the whole conversation, she realized that he said, "Once *we* get this taken care of," but there was no *we*. The fact was she got pregnant, not the other way around, and now the only way to go back to the way things were when she was cheerleader, scholarship student, talented, and beautiful was for her to fix this.

A tear slipped down her cheek, causing her teacher to ask, "Emma, are you okay?"

"Fine, Mrs. Kilmer. I …" She smiled, embarrassed.

After class was over, Mrs. Kilmer asked her again, this time in private. There was something about this caring teacher that made her want to open up, but she couldn't. There was too much at stake. Instead, she thanked her for her concern and left, but not before Mrs. Kilmer said, "I'm always here for you. Come in anytime if you need to talk." Emma had only nodded, knowing that that conversation would never take place.

***

"I've got something to tell you that you will never believe!" Eliza blurted enthusiastically.

"What?" Kate asked.

"Guess!"

Kate shrugged. She had a feeling she knew what Eliza was so pumped about, but she was also certain she didn't want to ruin it for her by guessing.

"My piece is getting published!"

"What? That's amazing!"

"Yeah. It's going out in this edition of our magazine."

"Congrats! What are we going to do to celebrate?"

"I have no idea. I'm too excited to think."

"You should tell Danny." A look of hesitancy crossed Eliza's beautiful features. "What is going on between you two?"

"Nothing. Why?"

"You two have been acting strange. Did something happen while I was in the hospital? Did you two make out or something?" Eliza's face turned a deep shade of red and then she laughed. "What is so funny?" Kate pleaded.

"He doesn't like me. What are you talking about?"

"You two are tip toeing around each other, and it's starting to get awkward." Eliza debated telling her friend the truth, but with all that was going on, she didn't think that Kate needed to set her straight. Eliza should be the one there for her.

"Stop it, Kate."

"I won't let this go, and you know it. Liza, fess up."

"There is absolutely nothing to tell. Nothing happened between us."

"If I didn't know better, I'd say he likes you."

"No, he doesn't. He likes you!" Eliza tried to cover up what she had just said, but all she managed to cover was her mouth. How dare she blurt out something so personal? If he liked her, he should tell her himself.

"How do you figure?"

"Did you see how he was with you in the hospital, all lovey and affectionate holding your hand, kissing you?"

"On the forehead. It sounds like maybe you are jealous."

"It's between you two. Leave me out of it."

"You like him."

Eliza looked at her friend. Her blue eyes locked with Kate's and seemed to speak the truth Eliza was

The Hope of Eliza

unable to utter herself. Of course, she liked him, and he liked her. Why had no one made a move?

"I was in the hospital. Of course, he was concerned for me. But to be honest, even though I was the one in physical danger, I think he worried about you the most."

"You don't like him?"

"As a friend, he is a very good friend, but no. I've never been attracted to him. Plus I'm not so into relationships right now. I think I'll pass on men for a while. I need time to figure things out on my own. But seriously, I called you two from day one."

"No, you didn't."

"Well, practically. I mean you both are smart, good-looking, have plans for your future, and are into God."

Eliza smiled. "Well, if all that is true, it still doesn't change the fact that he hasn't asked me out. Not only that, things have changed between us in a way I can't explain. That's why I think he likes you, and you deserve a really great guy."

"While that may be true, it's not him."

———

"Young, lady, come down here please."

"Yes, Mother," Emma called from her bedroom. Oh, what did she want? These days every encounter with her mother boasted some kind of discord. Bracing herself for controversy, she headed down the stairs.

"There you are. I need to speak with you. The mail came today. You know what arrived?"

"No idea, Mother." She sighed.

"Well, among the abundance of college advertisements, I found this." She held it out to her.

The white envelope no longer boasted pride and accomplishment. Emma looked down.

"What's the matter, dear? Don't you want to see them? Your father and I had some celebration plans for when this arrived." Emma couldn't speak. There was no need for celebration. "Emma," her mother said sternly, "I want an explanation. Three B's, one A, and several C's, and its less than halfway through the semester. Well, what do you have to say for yourself?" Her mother's face was livid at this point. Her slender hand was shaking from the pent up anger. "Well?" she demanded.

"I'm sorry, Mother," she started rather sincerely. "I've been distracted lately."

"*Distracted* is an understatement, don't you think? You have everything going for you in life: a nice car, plenty of friends, a charming boyfriend, that I haven't seen around much lately, all the clothes and shoes a girl could ask for, and all we ask is that you make good grades in school. Boy, we are really unreasonable parents, if you ask me. After all, good grades are so hard to achieve. You are a straight-A student, Emma. Really, what has come over you lately? You need to fix this."

All of the things in Emma seemed to snap at the same time. "I know, Mother!" she shouted. "Believe me: I know. I'll take care of it as soon as possible. You won't be bothered again." She snatched the envelope out of her mother's hand and stormed toward the stairs.

"Emma Marie! What has come over you? Get back here! You are in a load of trouble, young lady!"

The next few days only proceeded to be worse of the same. She had to do something. Luke was right. She was only procrastinating and making her life difficult. Maybe if she took care of this problem, she could relax. She took a deep breath and dialed the number to make an appointment. After hanging up the phone, she felt the first sign of relief in weeks.

Kate had been thinking. Eliza thought Danny liked her. She didn't get that sense at all. Well, there was only one way to find out.

"Hey, Danny, wait up. Where are you headed?"

"To the dorms to get some studying in. Why?"

"Do you have a sec?"

"Of course."

"Let me get straight to the point. You've been acting awkward around us ever since I got released from the hospital. Anything you'd like to share?" He looked puzzled, as though he was about to dodge the question. "Eliza …"

At that, Danny held a look of utter guiltiness, like he was a little boy caught with his hand in the cookie jar. "Look, don't you dare tell her, but I am starting to like Eliza." He spoke in a whispered tone, like it was top secret. Kate felt like she was back in middle school.

"So ask her out." His shocked expression told her he wasn't planning on it. "Why not?"

Hesitating once more, he fumbled for the right words. "Eliza is … special. She's not looking for just any guy. She's never dated or been with anyone before. It terrifies me how much I want this. I couldn't handle her saying no."

"Men!" Kate growled. "So let me get this straight: you don't want her to say no so you're not going to ask at all?"

"You act like that's absurd."

"Well, it is. Either way with this stupid plan of yours, you don't get to date Eliza. In the meantime, you run around like a fool while she thinks you're falling for another woman."

"What?"

"Oh no. I've helped you enough. Do you think by waiting longer your chances with her will increase?"

"I don't know."

"Well, think about it. This year your time together is guaranteed. Next year might not be like that."

"Kate, where are you going?"

"To ponder why I never get men …"

Danny laughed to himself. Kate was funny when she got all riled up. The best friend had just given him the okay. Did this mean Eliza liked him too? Danny never made important decisions fast. He decided he wouldn't be pressured by Kate's antics. Had she made up the part about Eliza thinking he liked someone else? Who could she possibly think he liked? He had felt a connection with Eliza at the hospital, but it never went anywhere. Now, he didn't know where to go from here. It felt like a big risk putting himself out there. If she said no, the rest of their year together would be ruined, but he didn't know if he could keep this strange game up any longer. He would ask her out … at the right moment of course. Whenever that would be.

Chapter 17

The relief was only short-lived. As the day of her appointment came closer, she wished more and more she didn't have to go. She heard it could be painful. What if someone saw her there? What if they all found out? She decided the only way she could make it through this would be if Luke went with her. If she had his support, she might find the courage to go and get it over with.

She picked up the phone hesitantly. Of course, he'd go. This wasn't just her problem. Luke didn't answer, and her appointment was just days away. Frustrated, she tried again.

This time, he answered in an annoyed voice. "What's up?"

"Are you busy or something? You didn't answer my call."

The Hope of Eliza

"I'm hanging out with the guys."

"Okay, well, I need to talk to you."

"Right now?"

"No, Luke, in person, in private. Can you come by this afternoon?"

"What? To your house?"

"Yeah. What's so bad about that?"

"Nothing, it's just that I haven't been there with your mom home since …"

"I know, and that's why you need to come. She's worried that you haven't been around."

"Really? Okay, never mind. Sure, I'll come see you later."

"Okay. And Luke?"

"Yes …"

"I love you."

"Me too. See you soon."

She smiled to herself. Everything would be all right.

Eliza finally worked up the courage to tell Danny her good news. She felt like a silly schoolgirl. Why was she so nervous? Well, for one thing, she didn't want him to think she was bragging. She couldn't predict his response either. What if he didn't think it was a big deal?

"Hey, Eliza."

"Hi, Danny."

"How's everything?"

"Great. Guess what. I'm getting my article on technology published."

"With Simmons?" he asked excitedly.

"Yep." He loved the way her eyes sparkled when she talked. Clearly, she was excited. It took him only a minute to summarize how he might use this situation. He could offer to take her out to celebrate. If she acted weird or hesitated, he could just play it off as a friend thing, but if she acted excited, he could …

"Congratulations," he said, giving her a big hug. "Hey, let's go out to celebrate."

"Okay. When?"

"How about tonight?"

"Great. I'll just let Kate know to be ready when you pick us up." Danny took a deep breath. This was not going his way. Eliza started down the hall.

"Eliza, wait."

"Yeah."

"I was kind of … Well, I was hoping that this time it could be … just the two of us?" He hated how unconfident he sounded, but he was all in now. Eliza grew quiet, and he wondered if he had made a mistake.

"Like a date?" she asked innocently.

Now he had to respond. He could pull the friend card or take a chance. "Yeah, kind of." Eliza smiled the biggest smile he had seen on her face lately, which made his risk seem like the right decision after all.

"Sure. See you tonight."

Eliza could barely contain her excitement as she walked out of sight. She couldn't wait to find Kate. *My goodness, what should I wear?*

When Luke came by, he seemed to be in a better mood. He hugged her and kissed her just like before. There seemed to be a softness in his voice. He ate dinner with her parents, discussed business with her dad, and complimented her mom on her cooking. Mom even seemed happier now that Luke was around. Pretty soon, her parents retired to their bedroom and she and Luke finally got a chance to talk.

"How are you doing?" he asked tenderly.

"I'm all right. I'm tired. I just wish this wasn't an issue."

How many times had Luke thought the same thing? Why did they have to be the ones to get pregnant? They had taken precautions, had practiced "safe sex." Not only that, they had been together only a few times, not even regularly. Now, they were faced with some rough choices with some terrible consequences. On the drive here, he'd had an imaginative moment where Mr. Steward had sat him down, told Emma to pack her things, and asked how he intended to provide for his daughter now that he had ruined her. It had been the worst nightmare of his life, and he had been awake!

"Me too, Emma. I'm so sorry."

She straightened and looked him straight in the eye. Her blue eyes became so intense he almost didn't recognize them. She had always been full of life, happy, and giddy. Today she was different. She faced him like a person ready to be hanged. Her despair and pain made him shiver. He was so afraid. Afraid of what would happen if she did go through with the procedure and terrified if she didn't. He had thought about it over and over. What would happen if she kept it? Luke would never tell Emma he had thought of anything else other than getting rid of it, because she was already clinging to hope when there was none. How much more would she consider it, if she knew he had entertained thoughts about how to proceed without the procedure? Of course, that wasn't even an option, but Emma was right. The choice seemed obvious, but not straightforward. Emotions could be tricky things.

"I need a huge favor." Her eyes changed from serious to seriously pleading in an instant. "Please go with me. I made an appointment, but I can't go unless you are there."

Luke didn't expect that. She was all but crying, and he hated when she cried. She had done it. Just

The Hope of Eliza

like that, she had an appointment. A relief filled him like it never had before. He wouldn't have to choose between Emma and his future. Going with her seemed like a small price to pay, so he quickly agreed. "Of course, I will, sweetheart. I'll go with you. I'll take care of you."

Emma released the breath she didn't know she had been holding. "Oh, thank you, Luke. I thought I could do it, but I'm just so scared."

"Don't worry. It'll all be over soon. When is the appointment?"

Eliza looked in the mirror. She had decided on a slim-fitting, red, cocktail dress. It was simple but had an elegant neckline and a halter. It was probably too formal, but even if they just went to Chili's, she wanted to make an impression. Kate had helped her get ready and put her hair up. The do was gorgeous with a bun and little ringlets of curls falling down. Liza only wore her hair like this for prom, so she hoped it would be fine.

She would definitely make an impression one way or the other. She sighed. "I might have gotten this whole situation wrong if he's not actually asking me out. What does 'sort of' a date mean?" She hoped she didn't overestimate his interest and embarrass herself. At the last minute, she decided to change into something cute but simple.

"Eliza, you can't. He'll be here any minute, and you look fabulous."

"So you can hold him off for a few minutes. I don't even know if he likes me."

"Trust me when I say guys don't ask girls out that they don't like."

"He could've been being nice because I got published."

Kate laughed. "Oh, Eliza. Lucky for you I know that is not the case." Eliza thought back to how he had specifically asked for it to be just the two of them. That did imply something. She was still undecided about whether to change when she heard a knock on the door.

"Here goes something," she said as she winked at Kate.

Eliza opened the door and took in the sight of him. He was wearing a nice pair of jeans with a gray button-up shirt. He had a suit jacket on. His dark hair was combed back and parted at just the right angle. What was more surprising than him getting dressed up was the alluring smell radiating from his body. He smelled so manly.

"Ms. Eliza, are you ready?"

"Yes, just let me grab my purse."

"Okay, but you won't need it." He smiled. Eliza figured he was implying that he would be paying, which was what she would expect even if this was just a "kind of" date.

"A girl always needs her purse, no matter the circumstance." Eliza glanced at Kate to tell her good-bye and then suddenly realized this was the first time since the incident that she had left Kate alone for more than a half an hour.

Kate, as if reading her thoughts, said, "Eliza, I'll be fine. Enjoy your date."

Eliza shook her head, laughing. Is that what all best friends did—read you like a book? "You could invite Annie over for a movie."

Kate indulged Eliza and smiled. "I could, or I can get this mountain of work done. Either way, I'll be perfectly safe, and I promise to ask someone if I need help."

"Okay. Have fun then."

"Will do. You guys too."

Emma started falling into a terrible depression she couldn't describe. Her mother was still in her high mood, but all that changed Tuesday morning when Emma couldn't get out of bed. She was probably still upset about the grades, but Emma didn't care. She couldn't go to school like this. Her mother angrily charged into her bedroom and yanked the covers off Emma. Emma had finally drifted off sometime after midnight, and when her alarm had gone off at 5:30, she had consciously shut it off. Slipping back into bed, she had thrown the covers over her head and vowed not to get up until noon. Now, her mother towered over her hands on her hips.

"What is wrong with you, Emma?"

"Mom, I'm sick," Emma croaked.

"Young lady, you look fine to me. If I were you, I'd get up out of bed and get ready so I can take you to school immediately. The longer you dawdle, the madder I'm going to get."

"I can't, Mom. I feel awful. I think I'm burning with a fever."

She leaned forward feeling Emma's head. "I think you're fine."

"Please, Mom."

She took one last look at her daughter. Emma's usual smile had disappeared; there were huge bags under her eyes. It looked like someone had drained the life out of her. She finally relented. "Today only, Emma. Tomorrow I expect you to be at school."

But Emma knew that what was really wrong wouldn't go away between now and then. After talking with Luke on Thursday, she had gained a strength she desperately needed. She had been fine for about four days. But the appointment was next Monday, and she was so scared she was shaking.

If they had been able to get the appointment last Friday, this all would have been over by now. She tried desperately to go back to sleep.

For the next several days, Emma wouldn't leave her bedroom. She wouldn't eat and couldn't sleep. She had no idea what was going on with her body. She felt immobilized and afraid. She barely answered Luke's texts when he asked why she wasn't at school. She had no idea why she wasn't at school. It was like her heart couldn't take any more emotions. It was going through war, and until one side won, it wasn't going to shut up. In the meantime, Emma felt like her heart was shriveling up because it wasn't getting the necessary things to live. "It is because I haven't been eating anything," she told herself.

By Thursday, her mother was ready to drag Emma to the emergency room. Emma protested the loudest she could, knowing she would be found out. If only she could hold on till Monday. Needless to say, she was "better" by Friday, determined she could make it through one more day of school. But when Luke saw her in the hallway and asked in a whisper if she was ready for Monday, something inside her snapped.

She ran from him! She ran down the hall and into the woman's bathroom, where she threw up. Her whole body was shaking. She had turned an unusual shade of white and couldn't stop wrenching, even though there was nothing left in her stomach.

She finally stopped, opening the door to find Jordyn staring at her.

Jordyn looked panicked. "Oh, honey, what's wrong?"

Emma burst into tears, no longer being able to control them. All the emotions she had packed carefully away were coming out.

After fifteen minutes of trying to regain control, Emma sniffed as she said, "Nothing. I'm just really sick, and Mom made me go to school."

"You should see a doctor."

"I know. Maybe I will."

"What's really bothering you?"

Emma looked at her best friend. Should she trust her? Jordyn could have half the school laughing through the rest of senior year. Though Emma knew deep down inside that that would never happen, she was afraid to tell her. "Luke and I aren't doing so well," she confided.

"Oh, honey, everyone goes through that. You and Luke were made for each other; it'll turn out all right. If this is about him not asking you to prom, I'll get his butt on it right away."

Emma laughed in spite of herself. Jordyn was a good friend. Even though she smelled like puke, her friend had her arm slung across Emma's shoulder in a protective, sisterly hug. Emma suddenly wished it were that easy to fix. Luke would ask her to prom and nothing would be wrong. Only that wasn't the issue. Emma realized she wasn't ready to go in for the procedure. She needed more time to get back to normal. She knew what she needed to do.

Danny pulled the chair out for Eliza. She looked good. The dress fit to her amazing curves, her blonde hair was curled, her smile was contagious, and her beautiful, brown eyes sparkled. He took these all as good signs. He breathed a sigh of relief. So far, so good.

Eliza was impressed. Danny opened every door and remembered all his manners. So this is what it felt like to be dating. She was elated. She felt like the whole world was glowing. She took in the sight of the restaurant, the smell of the food, the look on his face, and her own response to him.

"Congratulations, Eliza," he said smiling at her.

"Thanks. I'm excited. Finally, something goes right this year." A dark look crossed her face, and he instantly knew she was referring to all the things that had happened with Kate, but selfishly he didn't want to go there. He wanted Eliza's focus to be on the here and now. This was the first time she had left Kate's side. He wanted her to be happy and wanted to share in that happiness.

"Well, I think other things have been lining up, as well." Eliza glanced at him, trying to read whether he was referring to this date or not. She couldn't tell, so she just smiled.

He changed the subject abruptly. "I know Eliza, the dedicated reporter; I know Eliza, the loyal friend; but I feel like I need to know more about Eliza, the person."

Eliza had never thought of these things as separate portions of her life. His view was intriguing. Her the person—what could she say?

He laughed upon seeing the puzzlement on her face. She looked so cute. He could almost hear her thoughts by looking at her expressive facial features. "I bet you know a lot more than you're letting on. Tell me what you know, and I'll add to it."

"Fair enough. I know you're a dream chaser who doesn't give up. You're both a talented journalist and a hard worker. I've watched you, how you take care of others, how you care for others. I think you even have a soft spot for Josh when no one is looking. You are tender and kind and fun to be around."

Though what he said could have been coming from a friend, Eliza knew it was more than that. The way his voice settled low and sweet, his eye contact, and the admiration there told Eliza that he was serious about all he said. Her first thought was excitement; her second was panic. Was he about to ask her out? The sane part of her said that if he did, she would say yes. But there was another voice that spoke in her heart. It was the voice of an abandoned child who was assessing the potential risk of opening her heart to him. He seemed genuine, so Eliza could only trace her own fear back to her mother's story. She took a calming breath. Right now, she would choose to be part of this romantic story. She would face her fears for a chance to live her dreams.

"I have also seen your devotion to God and your passion for Him. How'd I do?"

"Pretty well. Yes, I'd say that about sums it up," she teased.

"Uh, uh. Not so easy; you promised to add."

"Well, what should I add to that masterfully spoken impression?" She was teasing again. He liked it when she let her guard down.

In the spirit of her lightheartedness, he asked, "Favorite color?"

"Oh, yeah, now we are getting to the deep, important things. Pink," she added. And then she burst out laughing, giving away that pink wasn't her favorite color.

"Let me guess … Green?" A shocked look registered on her face.

"How did you know?" she blurted. In truth, he didn't know. It was a guess—a good one, apparently.

"Well, green looks great on you. It complements your eyes." She blushed.

Now where had that comment come from? he thought sheepishly.

"Thanks. Yours?"

"Hmm?"

"Your favorite color?"

"Oh, dark blue."

"Uh, huh."

"Something amusing …"

"Well, you specified your shade."

"Yeah, well, there are a lot of blues: sky blue, dark blue, and girly blue. I didn't want you to be mistaken."

"Ha, ha …" She covered her mouth and continued to stifle her giggle. "Girl blue—that's a color I've never heard of. I know you are good with adjectives and all, but that was over the top."

"You think so? It just so happens that that blue is a very popular color and a guy has to protect his reputation."

Eliza couldn't hold it in anymore. Despite herself, she burst out laughing.

"What?" he said. "You know the color I'm talking about."

"I do, but most people just call it bright blue."

"If I didn't know any better, I'd say you were making fun of me."

"Oh no. I shouldn't. You might not ask me out on a second date then. She waited. Scarcely able to breathe, she scolded herself for going that far. Did it look like she was angling him for another date? She didn't even know what this first one meant yet.

"Since you brought it up, I'd like to ask you to go out with me to the movies Friday night."

Eliza straightened. As much as she was enjoying herself, she didn't want to shirk her duties to Kate.

As if reading her mind, he added, "Okay. I'd be willing to make it a group date, so long as you sit by me and hold my hand."

Eliza didn't know what to say. He was certainly forward about his feelings for her, but very unclear about where this was all going. She decided to feel it out by teasing him.

"Oh, I don't know. What would people say if we went on two dates? They might think there is something going on between us, you know what I mean?"

He smiled that gorgeous smile that had her all wrapped up. "What would they think was going on?"

She pretended to be angry. How silly of him to want to make her spell it all out. However, she couldn't refuse to answer, because she desperately wanted to know. "They might think instead of a casual date that you actually like me a lot."

He paused, studying her with his handsome face, and answered, "So what if they do?"

"I just don't want to give them any wrong impressions, because I still don't know what exactly you are proposing."

Eliza expected him to beat around the bush more with this silly banter, but instead, he looked her in the eye and said, "I'll be entirely honest then. I do really like you. In fact, I've been wanting to ask you out since the hospital hallway, but I was ... I didn't want you to say no. Now that you agreed, I didn't want to make things too serious on our first date, but since your curiosity has gotten the better of you, I'll take the plunge. Eliza, will you go out with me?" He couldn't believe he had just asked her. A gentleman would never do that on the first date. They hardly knew each other in this "liking" stage.

He felt like all the air had been extinguished from his lungs as he waited for her response.

Eliza was outwardly composed and inwardly freaking out. How should she respond? "I think ... Yes, I would like that." How silly she sounded, even to herself. You could definitely tell all this was new to her, but it didn't seem to matter to him. He looked and sounded even less composed. The way he was attempting to sit still reminded Eliza of a three-year-old waiting to tear into the wrapping paper.

Taking her hand from across the table, he pressed it to his lips. "You have just made my day," he said.

Shesmiled. "Let's go on a walk." Eliza could think of nothing better. She had a ton of things on her mind. Mostly, what would dating Danny be like?

"You what? Emma, how could you?" Emma was shocked at Luke's reaction. Directly after placing a call to the center and telling them she needed more time, Emma had felt a relief she hadn't felt in the last four days. She expected Luke to be disappointed, not angry. "Emma, you're just postponing the inevitable and making us both miserable."

That was the last straw for Emma. Him miserable! Her several weeks pregnant, having to go through a painful operation to keep their secret, and poor Luke miserable. "You jerk. You never care how I feel. It's all about you, isn't it? Well, let me tell you something. You're not the one taking flak from your parents, your teachers, your friends. You're not tired to death. You're not the one who's throwing up, and you're not the one that they have to go inside of to fix the problem. So forgive me if I'm scared. I can't do it right now, Luke. I'll do it, but right now, I've never been more miserable in my whole dang life!"

"I know, and you will be until you go. Please reschedule the …"

But Emma had already hung up. "What a heartless … cruel … Uhhhh!" He made her so angry. She would schedule it when she was good and ready.

Emma didn't see or talk to Luke all weekend except briefly at the baseball game, but Emma told herself it was a good thing. She didn't need his emotions right now. She had enough of her own. She did feel slightly guilty when Luke got taken out of the game though. Usually one of their best hitters, he had struck out the first three times at bat. The team had ended up losing by twelve points. Oh, well. At least he finally understood part of how she felt. However, Monday she dreaded facing him more than anything. She hoped it would have smoothed over during the course of the weekend, but one look at his face, and she knew that it hadn't.

"Hello, sweetheart," Emma greeted cheerily.

"We need to talk."

"Okay. Where?"

"Let's go out for lunch. We can sit in my car."

"Okay. Just let me grab my purse." Emma climbed in the Camaro more nervous than ever. She half-wished he would start making out with her and apologizing, but she didn't hold out much hope for that.

"What's on your mind, *Luke?*"

"Look, Emma. I know this is hard for you. I know you think you're the only one going through it, but that isn't the truth. If you keep this up …"

"Luke, calm down. I'm not going to keep it. I'm not stupid."

"Then why delay? Why make us both miserable? We can't sleep, our parents wonder what's wrong with us, my coach is frustrated to death, your grades are sinking, and you're throwing up in the bathroom—"

"How did you know about all that? Have you been talking to Jordyn behind my back?"

"No, everyone's worried about you."

"Don't give me that, Luke. You don't seem concerned. It's all so simple to you, right? Just go. Get it done! I don't even know what they are going to do to me in there. I'm scared. And all you care about is yourself. I'm sick of it."

"Emma, we're both on the line here. Do you think no one is going to catch on? You may start showing soon. Our friends know something's up, and you're mom is not an idiot. If she would have taken you to the doctor, it would have been over. And it's not just you, Emma. Do you think anyone will be stupid enough to believe it's someone else's? Think about it. We've been going out for two years. Yes, I remembered it was our anniversary too. Look, Emma, this is hard. Aren't you tired of it?"

"Yes, but I need more time Luke. Not a long time. Just maybe a week or so."

"I'm sorry, Emma, but I can't wait that long. Look at me. Have you ever seen me this miserable? Did you see my game performance? And I hate seeing you like this. I can't take it anymore. You make me want to cry every time I look at you."

"I'm sorry I'm such a reminder of what we chose to do. You're just going to have to get over it, Luke Howard. This is my decision, not yours. I'm the one who's pregnant, remember? It's my body."

"And it's our life. I'm sorry, Emma, but I can't see you till you've done this. I'll be waiting for you afterwards."

Emma's draw dropped. "How dare you leave me, Luke! You're the one who got us here in the first place, *and now it's my problem?*"

Emma grabbed the first thing she saw in the car, his glasses, and chucked them at him full force. "I hate you, Luke Howard! Don't ever touch me again!" She flung open the car door and started running back into school.

Stopping, she decided she didn't want to go there. She crossed over, got into her own car, and peeled out of the parking lot. She had no idea where she was going.

Time seemed to fly by for Eliza. She was crazy busy with school, with work, with friends, and of course, with Danny. She couldn't believe that the internship was almost over. Danny had become her best friend in the entire world. He was so quick to love her, spoil her, and compliment her. They could talk for hours about God, school, their dreams, their plans, and their futures. It didn't take Eliza long to realize this could be the "one" she was looking for. He was romantic. The way he kissed, snuggled, and held her gave her a glimpse of what it might be like to be married to this man, but as promised, he never pushed Eliza's physical boundaries. So in fact, she had found a man who was willing to wait. He had even taken some of his Christmas break to spend with Eliza's family and Kate, of course.

Kate was more like a sister now. They shared things that Eliza would never have dreamed about sharing with anyone before. Her mom had become Kate's mom, which was ironic because Grammy had been Mom's adopted mother. Her whole family, though a little out of the ordinary, seemed like it was sewn together and planned since the beginning of time. So far, the only problem was there wasn't a man in the family. *But that might change soon,* she thought giddily.

Eliza also, got to visit Danny's family over spring break. They made her feel so welcomed and loved. His mom was a natural hostess. His younger sister was dying to have an ally in a "house full of boys," as she called it. Danny had two younger twin brothers. At age twelve, they were extremely active and super cute. Eliza had grown up as an only child, so sibling relationships were new to her. She carefully watched their interactions with each other. They were playful, loving, and teased each other a whole lot. They sometimes argued over little things, but in the end, they couldn't stand to be angry with one another. Eliza thought she probably had it easy in that department. She had never had to get along with anyone. It was naturally very easy to get along with your mom, especially Eliza's mom, and there was no one else to have to get along with. She thought their family was very charming, and even the children were exceptionally well behaved.

The best and worst part of the whole trip was watching the interactions between his parents. They too teased each other, laughed with each other, and even were publicly affectionate in a sweet way. The way Mr. Robertson held his wife's hand when they prayed at the table, the way he sporadically twirled her around the kitchen, the way he gently kissed her or hugged her—all of this Eliza now missed. Questions started to arise: Did my mom ever want more than just one kid? Does she ever feel lonely? Doesn't she want what I now have: a constant friend, a true love? Did she give that up too while she raised me?

The Hope of Eliza

    The way Mr. Robertson interacted with his daughter Connie was also a mystery. Eliza had seen this growing up but never in a home environment. The way he hugged her, chased her, tickled her, teased her, and talked with her seemed out of this world. It was like his world had two centers: his wife and his daughter. Of course, there were the three boys as well, but Eliza could tell there was something special about a father-daughter relationship.

    She also saw it in Connie's self-image. The girl was humble but also solid. She knew her value. She never had to prove her beauty with low-cut tops or heavy makeup. She was confident, which added to the beauty of her long, dark, curly hair and her bright smile. She was so … innocent? Protected? She had true joy that spread throughout the entire house. She was great with the twins too. She always came up with some game or fun activity in which she often participated in. Once, she got the whole family, even Mr. and Mrs. Robertson, to ride mattresses down the stairs inside their house! Nothing so disorderly had ever happened or been planned in Eliza's home. She laughed. "So this is what a 'house full of boys' means."

    Eliza and Danny had talked about a future together one day. He seemed insistent that they would be able to work out whatever change happened after graduation. "We'll be together," he promised.

However, the closer they got to graduation, the more nervous Eliza had become. She had learned a lot about herself in the dating process. One thing she had learned was that, for no explainable reason, she had a hard time trusting people, especially the men in her life. The more she thought and prayed about it, the more she traced it back to a simple thing. Her father had left her before she even knew him. His leaving somehow had affected her more than she had realized all these years. Eliza knew in her heart that Danny was trustworthy, but she doubted him all the same. Would they really remain together? What if circumstances pushed them in opposite directions? She tried not to dwell on these things because they only wanted to shatter her heart. Graduation was only one week away. Finals were this week, and she had to be focused.

Family was coming into town Friday night, including his entire family and her mom and Grammy. Eliza couldn't wait to see them. Mom and Grammy had driven up once this last semester, but that seemed like ages ago. Her internship was over. The company was looking to hire a few interns to continue the work they had started.

The great thing about the job was that Simmons expected them to continue their education at the college. It was an almost full-time position with a really nice starting salary. Eliza was determined to stay even if she didn't get the job; she wanted to finish at this college.

Kate was considering transferring to be closer to her sister, but that depended on her ability to find a job. The ideal situation would be to stay on at Simmons and finish her education. But it all depended on the announcements made at graduation. Some of the interns had already been proactive about looking for jobs outside Simmons. John (aka Mr. Grant Jr.) had already applied and been offered a position. He had lots of options but decided on working for a scientific inventions company that wanted a professional to publish articles related to its advancements in technology and scientific experiments. The company also wanted him to collect data and do research analysis. His papers would likely affect how the product was manufactured, based on his scientific observations.

Eliza was happy for him but knew that never in a million years did she want to go into research development. She still had her heart set on journalism. She was waiting to hear Mr. Grant's announcements and figured she had all summer to find a job to help her with her educational expenses. Next Saturday would be very interesting.

Emma couldn't stop crying. She drove as far and as fast as she could till she realized that she couldn't see the road clearly because of her tears. So she just pulled over on a quiet freeway sightseeing exit and beat the steering wheel until her hands turned blue from the self-inflicted bruises, which just made her angrier. She cussed and bawled and threatened Luke for over two hours until all the anger had vanished and a broken heart took residence. She tried to tell herself that Luke would never leave her. They were supposed to be together. They *would be* together. She felt like she wanted to die. Now she had the courage she had lacked before. She had no other choices left to battle with. She drove home dejected and alone.

As Luke promised, they didn't see each other anymore. The only times she ever heard from him were brief meetings in the hall and a text message that read "I'll be waiting for you."

"I have great news for you, Eliza," Danny said, rushing up to her.

"You already know about your job at Simmons?" It was Saturday morning, the day of graduation, and Eliza could think of nothing else that would interest him more.

"No, no one knows that, but I do know that I have an interview for another internship in town." Eliza waited and begged him with his eyes to hurry up and continue already. "I think they might offer me the position."

"Which one is this?"

Danny had been applying for all of the local jobs so that he and Eliza would have a chance at staying in the same place after graduating Simmons. Eliza had no idea which one he was so excited about.

"You know the internship with the political news station that promises a job after graduating the program." Eliza gasped; this was his dream job. Politics and journalism had always been Danny's main pursuits. These were topics usually too controversial for Simmons Publishing Corporation as a whole, but Danny had received a lot of positive feedback from Mr. Grant, who believed Danny had the makings of an incredible journalist.

He had made a similar statement about Eliza; however, Eliza's pieces focused more on the humanitarian side of things and were more on level with what Simmons often published. "That's great!" she exclaimed.

"It's not like a regular internship. It's an actual job—a paid internship. That's not the best part!"

"What?"

"It's only ten minutes from the college, and that would mean we don't have to have our relationship long distance." Eliza couldn't believe what she was hearing. She tried not to get her hopes up and get caught up in his enthusiasm. It was hard hearing how excited he was and how sure he was that he would get the job.

"Already, I've passed through the first three steps of the interview process. I think they are really serious. I think they are looking to hire me."

"I hope so, Danny. How many others are they interviewing?"

"I have no idea. I just wanted to tell you the good news first before I tell Mom and Dad."

Eliza kissed him surely on the lips. He thought of her first. He was so sweet. He was determined they stay together and not move to different cities, and she was determined to stay here to finish school. This would efficiently solve the dilemma if he got the job. He seemed confident, and she was confident of his abilities. She only hoped they wouldn't choose someone older with a better resume. Simmons would look good, but these were two very different areas of journalism. Danny squeezed her tightly and rushed off to tell his parents the good news.

Walking across the Simmons stage meant more to Eliza than her four-year graduation might. Simmons had stretched her abilities and pushed her limits in a way that no class thus far had done. Plus she had accomplished much more here. Even though editing wasn't glamorous, her work had counted for something. The work she edited was now in print, as were some of her own pieces. This was what she wanted to do with her life.

The graduation was nice. It was set up in the same room they had entered nearly nine months ago. The room hadn't changed much, but the interns had. They had all bonded and become a tight-knit team. They had worked together, fought together, laughed together, and cried together.

The room itself was decorated for the occasion. The interns got to sit up on the stage in chairs facing the audience. Many family members and friends packed the auditorium, which boasted bright balloons set up randomly around the room. Also, refreshment tables had been brought in. They showed off a huge congratulations cake, some punch, mini desserts, and coffee. Curtains that were hung up on poles served as a backdrop behind the stage, offering more colors of celebration.

The graduates themselves were dressed up—formal attire only. Each one possessed a proud smile. Mr. Grant made a general announcement.

"Good afternoon, everyone. I am so glad you could make it to celebrate these fine interns' accomplishments. Each one of them deserves to be standing, or rather sitting, on this stage. They have worked hard, improved more than I can say, and helped make this company a continued success. I am proud of this class, who together published twenty pieces either in our magazine or in local newspapers. They have edited—I don't know how many pieces. Too many for me to count, I assure you. They have done countless hours of research, turned in too many assignments, have accepted and acted on feedback from professionals in their field, and have made this company proud. I can't wait to see where this class goes from here and what they will accomplish. So without further ado …"

Mr. Grant proceeded to call each intern forward and say something about each "journalist," as he now called them. Then he handed them their diploma and a wrapped gift from the Simmons Company as well as a recommendation letter for future endeavors. All precious gifts. These were followed by expressive cheering from the stage and the audience as each one shook hands with Mr. Grant—some of them hugging him.

When all this had come to a close, Mr. Grant joined them in their huddle for a group picture and then walked back to the podium as the graduates took their seats next to family and friends. "One last announcement, the one you've all been waiting for: who the recipients of a job at Simmons are. Please understand that being offered this job does not mean that you have to accept, of course. Also, you are all deserving candidates. If you do not receive a job offer at this time and are still interested in working here, please keep us in mind as you go forward. I'm not looking to fill a specific number of open spots, but I'm looking for people who could fill current roles where we need more support. Therefore, I will not be offering more jobs if people turn down their job offer, but everyone is welcome to apply in the future.

"I would like to offer our first job position to Miss Annie Whitfield, who has been working with one of our current authors and has very much met her expectations in every way."

Eliza's stomach became heavy. Sitting with her mom and holding her hand, she could only hope and pray that she had earned the right to be here.

Once the applause died down, he spoke again. "The second, I would like to award to a well-deserving candidate whose work ethic and genuine personality makes her a pleasure to work with, Miss Eliza Steward."

Eliza couldn't believe her ears. She got up on shaky legs as her friends and both families applauded and screamed her name. She shook hands with Mr. Grant and thanked him.

Returning to her seat, she began listening for other familiar names. "The third award goes to Miss Kate Beckett. She is a deserving recipient because of her skill and knowledge of the field. Kate will make a great asset to this team.

"Oh man, this is hard. I want to offer you all jobs." A polite chuckle escaped the audience. "Our fourth award goes to Jim Everfields, who has worked tirelessly and shows great enthusiasm with everything he does at Simmons." Jim accepted the award with a broad smile on his face, as he shook hands with Mr. Grant.

"Last but not least, Josh Johnson, whose enthusiasm and natural people skills will push him far in his career. Congratulations, Josh."

Eliza was concerned. She glanced at Kate, whose smile held a mixture of admiration and nervousness. Eliza had noticed the change in him, and he was always very good at his internship role, so Eliza was unsure why she was surprised that he got the job. But she was. She clapped anyway.

When the applause died down, he continued. "I would like to say a few words about John Miller, who would have been offered a job but has already told me that he has been hired at Adelphia, which is a prestigious research company. John is brilliant, detailed, and amazing at what he does. We wish him the best."

He paused as everyone clapped for John, and then he wrapped it up by saying, "Good luck to all the graduates. Have a great summer, and I hope to be reading your future pieces soon."

The crowd shouted, clapped, and stood up. Hugs were being passed around. Eliza hugged Grammy and her mother and then looked for Danny. She didn't spot him until it was almost too late. Having found her, he rushed to her side, scooped her up, and twirled her, kissing her with delight.

"You did it! You got the job!" He set her down but didn't let her go. "I love you."

"And I love you, Danny." Kate waited patiently before clearing her throat and rushing to congratulate Eliza.

"You too, Kate. Yay! We will be working together."

"Well, we'll at least be working in the same building."

"Oh, Eliza we are so very proud of you. Danny's family has invited us all out to a celebration dinner. Would you two girls be interested?" Kate and Eliza smiled at each other and then back at Eliza's mom.

"Of course, we would!" Kate almost shouted just to tease Eliza.

Just then, Josh sauntered up, looking a little embarrassed. "Congratulations, Kate, Eliza." Then to Kate, he said, "It looks like we will be seeing more of each other."

"Congratulations," both girls said, and Kate reached for a hug. Josh smiled sincerely and looked like he had trouble releasing Kate from his arms.

Eliza couldn't help but ask, "Do you want to go to lunch with all of us?"

"Thanks, Eliza, but my family is here."

"Okay, see you around."

"You two ladies, have a good day."

Eliza looked at Kate's face. She looked stunned that Eliza had asked him to join them but also showed a hint of disappointment that Josh couldn't make it.

This could get interesting, Eliza thought. Eliza gave Kate another big hug and the two talked nonstop all the way to the restaurant.

Eliza braced herself for the surprise that she knew would be awaiting Kate once they were seated. It was her graduation gift to her best friend.

"Kate!" A little girl about ten years old ran wildly toward her sister.

"Oh my goodness! Carolyn!" Kate couldn't stop the tears that fell as she embraced her sister. She couldn't let her go. The Petersons waited patiently before introducing themselves as Carolyn's mom and dad. Kate embraced the mom, Jennifer Peterson, and shook hands with the dad, Larry Peterson. It was the perfect family reunion. Eliza had a feeling that Kate might have Carolyn as the center of her attention for the day, but Eliza had no problems with that seeing the joy on Kate's face.

Sitting alone in the cold, sterile environment, Emma tried to make herself comfortable. The nurse was nice enough, and she even assured her that she wouldn't have to wait long. A good thing, considering she already wanted to bolt.

Life was so unfair. Why was she sitting alone? She knew why. Luke had flaked on her said he couldn't afford to miss school. Besides, it might look suspicious if they were both absent. Already, she was going to be in deep trouble for ditching. She hadn't thought of a good explanation to tell her parents, and she was too tired to care. She'd probably just collapse on the couch and pretend she had come home sick and forgotten to have them call her out. They might get upset, but ultimately, they would forgive her. Skipping was forgivable, but not this. This could only be fixed one way.

She could almost hear Luke's voice. "It's okay, baby. After this is over, everything will go back to normal and we can be happy again. You're just a little emotional. Besides, it wasn't our fault. We did everything we could to prevent this pregnancy. We're too young; we don't have a choice."

That had been their only descent discussion in the last two weeks. They only spoke because Emma needed to tell him about the appointment.

She took a deep breath. Some fleeting and uninvited thought suddenly overcame her heart, nearly bringing her to tears. "What would I name the baby?" The question so seized her heart that she quickly brushed away the tears and repositioned herself on the cold chair. Outwardly, she appeared the same as before, but inwardly, she knew the damage had been done. "Eliza," she whispered. "That's what I would name her."

She didn't know how this thing inside her was a baby girl, but somehow she unmistakably believed, whether through instinct or something else, that the baby was a girl. But she quickly reminded herself this thing was not a baby. Besides, even if she could have the child, her life would be ruined. No college, no resources, no money, and no husband. What kind of life would that be anyway? Surely, whatever was inside her would not want to enter such a cruel world.

Besides, she would be alone. Luke would never speak to her. He had said as much during one of their many fights that had followed that day he broke up with her. And her parents, if they ever spoke to her again, would be harsh, unforgiving, and spiteful because she had ruined their fairy-tale lives—their family "image," as they would put it.

Her palms grew sweaty as she remembered a country song where a teenager called his girlfriend while she was in a waiting room just like this and said he was wrong and that they should get married and raise their child.

This thought immediately brought huge tears that could no longer be held back. She was glad she was alone in the waiting room. Sobs that were uncontrollable escaped her pale lips. She held herself and asked the ever-haunting question: *Why did this happen to me? We took precautions, practiced safe sex, and yet look at me!* Unconsciously, she placed her hand on her small belly. Just beginning to form, she had been able to hide the ugly truth. Her parents and friends all asked if she was okay; some even commented that she looked as if she had gained a few pounds. Everyone asked, except Luke. He knew. They were in this together. It was their secret burden and stress.

Or was it? If that was the case, where was he? Was he too ashamed to sit in front of the doctors and say, "I'm the one who got her pregnant"? Or was he nervous someone might recognize him? It was different for the father. He could walk away. Emma knew she'd never be able to walk away, not even after today. Like it or not, she was attached to this thing that was forming inside her. She wanted it gone, but she was scared. Could she really do it? If only she could already be done, then things would go back to normal.

"Are you ready to come in now, my dear?" the doctor asked. He offered a relaxed smile as only doctors could pull off under the extreme circumstances they worked in every day. Emma just stared back, not answering. Her whole body shook with fear, yet she was doing the right thing.

She finally stood up on shaky legs. She glanced around the tiny waiting room one last time. She willed herself to move her feet, but they would not. Was she that afraid of the pain?

She glanced nervously at the doctor before resting her hands on her semi-formed belly. How could life be this cruel? She had dreamed of being pregnant, and how many times had she rested her hand on her stomach, gently massaging it when she was young? Even before Luke, she had dreamed of being a mother. Maybe it was some womanly intuition or something. She didn't know, nor did she care at the moment. Right now, all she knew was for the first time she could feel some sense of connection with this organism that was inside her.

Was this what it would have felt like all along if her life wasn't such a mess? She had always imagined being a mother, but not now. Not like this. She had never imagined the moment quite like this. Instead of excitement, she was filled with shame. Instead of a handsome father rejoicing, it was a quick-skip boyfriend who was only too happy not to have to deal with the inconvenience. Yet he loved her, right? That is why he had promised to come back to her as soon as this was all over.

She took a deep breath and moved forward slowly. A panic rose inside her. This was her last chance to have this over with. Whatever she chose in this moment, she would see it through. No more going back and forth. Her feet slowed, and then she stood still—perfectly still.

What should I do?

Emma and Eliza's Epilogue

What Might Happen if Emma Chooses to Have Her Baby

Emma took a ragged breath. She didn't want to relive this scene with her daughter, but she knew the reporter in Eliza wanted and needed the truth. For so long, she had sheltered her daughter from her story. She didn't want Eliza to have to experience the pain. She never wanted her daughter to feel responsible for Luke's and her parents' abandonment. Eliza was her everything, but would she see it that way?

How could Eliza ever forgive them for turning their heart away from their own flesh and blood? But it was time. She needed to trust Eliza with the entire truth.

Emma closed her eyes. She remembered the angry scene as if it were yesterday.

"*You're pregnant?* We are going to get this taken care of right now, Emma Marie Steward!"

"No, we're not."

"What?" Her mom was livid. "I wish your dad was here to talk some sense into you, Emma! What are you going to do? Keep it?" Emma had remained silent. "I'm done raising kids, Emma. How could you be so stupid?"

"Didn't you want Luke and me to give you grandkids?"

Her mother's eyes snapped. "Grandkids, yes! Not this despicable crap. That thing is a mistake!"

Emma melted into tears. "Well, it's not yours." Emma knew she had pushed her mother over the edge with that comment, but she meant it—every word.

"Emma Steward, you may not keep it. End of story."

"No, Mother, it's not. I am going to be responsible."

"And Luke?"

Emma couldn't look at her.

"I see ... I always knew he was the reasonable one. You emotional, selfish girl are going to end all of our lives. Well, I won't have it. You and I are going to the hospital now."

"I won't. I've tried, but ..."

"Emma, it's not a choice."

"You can't make me."

"You unreasonable, selfish brat! You either go with me right now or get out of my house."

Emma had turned without another word, slamming the door on the way out. She thought her mother would come around once she cooled off, but after being kicked out, she never returned "home."

Her life would have taken more miserable turns had it not been for Jordyn and, more surprisingly,

Jordyn's mom. Jordyn's mom had loved her like her own daughter. Later, after the baby had arrived, in the hospital she met an elderly woman called "Grammy." She got to know Emma and for the first time didn't look at her with judgment, as so many others had done. This mom had saved her life, brought her to the church, and given her a home and a new family. She had been the emotional support Emma had needed to stand on her own without Luke and without her parents. She had never seen her father again. She sent photos and cards but never heard a word. Emma figured that for her dad it was too painful to see her without being able to protect her and invite her back home, which he would never do without her mother's okay. She hadn't heard from Luke after Eliza was born. Last she heard, he denied that it was his baby and claimed that was why they had been having problems.

Emma found her life in Eliza. The way she smiled, the calendar documenting all of her firsts: first time rolling over, first time sitting up, first time crawling, first time walking … Those were her moments of joy.

Sometimes, Eliza reminded her of Luke. Her brown eyes, her laughter, her athleticism, and her eagerness to become somebody all screamed Luke. Emma would have never moved on, had it not been for her beautiful baby girl who needed her so much. Though her life had been hard, she never regretted giving Eliza life. But she knew she would have always regretted taking away Eliza's hope for life and the pursuit of happiness.

※

The journalist in Eliza couldn't let her past go unanswered. Her mother finally told her what had really happened all those years ago. She was amazed at all her mother went through to keep her. She was also shocked to know how close she was to never being born. What would have happened to all of them if she hadn't been born? Would Mom and Grammy have ever met? Would Danny have ever married? Would Luke still be with her mom? What would have happened to Kate? So many questions remained unanswered, so she found the one person that she thought could fill in all the pieces: her dad.

Eliza was angry at him. She wanted to prove to him that she deserved this life she had and to prove how wrong he had been. But once she had finally tracked him down, she realized something very important. He didn't hold her answers. He wasn't part of her life.

Looking around her, she saw a strange little family: Danny and their children, Grammy and Mom, the Robertsons, the Becketts, and the

Petersons. Her little family had grown so much over the past few years, and God had provided the healing that they all needed to move on. It hit her. This was all she wanted, all she needed; this was who she was.

If Luke had stayed, she wouldn't be this person. Somehow with his influence, she would have been different. Better or worse? She didn't know. But she no longer had the idea to meet with him, because to her, it was the ones that had stuck by her all those years that meant the most. She didn't want or need anyone else. Luke had made his choice, and she was making hers.

In her lifetime, Eliza did become a published author. Her work is not well-known, but she is nevertheless a success. She writes on many topics but is most passionate about real people who have overcome difficulties in life. She published a piece on her mom, Emma, who had become a single parent in high school. She wrote an unpublished piece about her adopted grandmother, the only one she'd ever really known, a women who was willing to shelter a lost soul who had been shunned by her family. She wrote about a woman from Nigeria who was self-educated and then taught her siblings and eventually started a school in her hometown. Eliza published a story about a little boy who miraculously recovered from leukemia.

To this day, she has written hundreds of unpublished stories that she hopes to compile into a large book about the compassion of the human heart. She is considering the title *Pebbles in the Water: How We Touch Each Other's Lives*.

She lives near her mother in her hometown. Though she doesn't have contact with her father, she finally found a man who was willing to wait: Danny. For her children, he became the dad she never had. She has three kids and works for a local magazine. Eliza and Kate are still very close.

Though her life is rather ordinary, Eliza is an extremely beautiful person on the inside and out. There are so many lives that she has touched in such small ways that she may never know them all. But for one person in particular, she was the difference between life and death.

Dear Readers,

Thank you so much for reading my book. I hope you enjoyed your experience. If this story has inspired you, please let me know by visiting my website: www.tawnyekanumuri.com. I would love to hear from you.

Sincerely,
Tawnye Kanumuri

Dear Unwed Mother,

You are my Emma and my hero, whose decision to bring your child into this world has impacted thousands of people. Thank you for withstanding the shame, for sacrificing so much for your child either by giving it up for adoption or by raising your baby. Thank you for being strong. I apologize for the judgment that has been passed upon you. You had a choice, one that appeared to fix everything, but you chose life. Jesus said, "Let any one of you who is without sin be the first to throw a stone at her" (John 8:7). I admire your courage and strength.

Love,
Tawnye Kanumuri

To My Fellow Pro-Lifers,

Find a way to support the Emmas out there, and you will find the way to save their children. Have compassion as Jesus had compassion. Love the people around you, despite their mistakes or maybe because of them. Abortion is wrong, but the only way to change a wrong is to reach the human heart for Jesus.

This book is dedicated to all my Emmas.

This book was founded on the premise that abortion has countless victims but that there are two primary victims: the baby and the mother. This book was written for the mother of the baby. This book was written for the scared, helpless girls who are confused and panicked. This book gives them a voice.

It was also written for her child, the one whose very life hangs in the balance.

Society sees being pregnant out of wedlock as shameful. While I believe this isn't God's perfect plan, I see this girl as a hero. She selflessly puts her life on hold, puts her own dreams aside, and takes responsibility for her and her man's choice. The mother is the only one who physically carries the shame. Everyone knows her or think they know her because they can identify her. Her pregnancy is like a scarlet letter proclaiming to all, strangers and friends alike, what she has done. All too often, the truth is this: society scorns her. Society rarely scorns "them," because in situations like these, there usually is no "them." It's her. She got pregnant. She slept with him. How dare she!

The father doesn't carry the physical sign of their indiscretion with him. It may have been his idea, but no stranger is ever going to know. Sometimes, he never knows about the baby born of their indiscretions and sin. Even if he takes responsibility, he is often unequipped with the notion on how to be a support to his girl and their baby. Also, it will still never be the same for him, because society holds this idea that men are just men after all. And that somehow puts most of the responsibility for keeping a relationship sexually pure on the women. This is not biblical. In fact, God is clear that He has high expectations when it comes to leadership.

The father, of course, has his own consequences. But when it comes down to it, in most cases, the mother suffers more judgment and takes more responsibility for the situation because she has to, because she is the only one who is pregnant.

Who cares for, suffers with, and carries the burden of raising a child alone? She does. She who chooses life suffers the consequences.

In this world we live in, there is sometimes no support for these moms. They drop out of high school because of the shame. Their friends (though they also sleep around) desert them. Their "boyfriends" often abandon them, not taking the responsibility toward her or the child. Financially, she falls victim to poverty with no means for higher education. She may only have one saving grace: her family. But often, even this is a dead-end road for her.

Put yourself in her shoes. Hear her tears and her broken heart. What would it feel like to expose yourself to the people you love and adore? How could you tell them if you had done something awful? What would you do for those nine months? What would you do after that? How would you survive?

And then, what if nobody had to know about it? What if it could all go away? You tell yourself, "I could finish school and make this right down the road. I could change. I wouldn't have to confess and break their hearts. They wouldn't have to know how I've let them down. I wouldn't lose him. I wouldn't be the laughingstock of the school, my job, or my family. I wouldn't have to be a mom at sixteen. What could I even offer a child? I can't keep it. I have nowhere to go. I couldn't provide for it. Besides, it's not a baby yet. I have a way to fix this. Nobody has to know ..."

And that is where the lie starts. It's the beginning of the destruction. That decision takes the baby's life, but that choice haunts and destroys the girl. It's not true that it will go away. She will always regret and blame herself for what she has done. She won't be compassionate toward herself. She will grieve the first time she brings life into the world. She'll be separated from her spouse by the lies she's been telling herself all these years.

Studies from both sides try to put a number on exactly how many women regret their abortions. But looking at the human heart, at the heart of a mother, I would say that, even if they don't admit it even to themselves, that number is very high. Their suffering begins the moment they realize the truth. They hate that part of themselves and don't know how to fix it anymore, but there is hope. Through Christ Jesus, we have been forgiven. All of us have been forgiven for all of our sins. We don't have to keep paying for our mistakes. That is one of the greatest lies of the Devil. He will tell you to keep punishing yourself and that you deserve it. That last part may seem true to us, but only if we ignore the sacrifice and what Jesus has paid for our freedom. We owe it to Him to let Him heal the wounded parts of our heart so that we can be free.

Because in freedom, we are free to approach His throne room. We gain a relationship with Him that can't be replaced by anything else in this world. But if we hang onto our guilt, we keep ourselves from coming to Him and in doing so resign ourselves to a life of self-imprisoned misery which we cannot escape.

No matter what choice you made, you are sought after by the King of Kings, God, Emmanuel. He wants to heal your broken heart. He will wipe your tears. He will help you get up. He has paid our debt and taken away all our guilt. I am sorry that you felt alone when you were pregnant, but He was, and always is, with you. He suffers with you, longing to gather you in His arms as a hen gathers her chicks beneath her wings (Matthew 23:27). His arms are reaching for you. Reach back to Him. He will shield you in His strength, in His warm, strong, kind embrace. His love for you is endless! You are His treasured one, and He longs for you to be His. I promise He is kind and gentle, not like some of the fathers and mothers and friends of this world. He will never leave you and never push you away.

> God loves you unconditionally.
> God loves you sacrificially.
> God understands you intimately.
> God relates to you continually.

These words were spoken by a pastor. I wrote them in my Bible to remind me of their truth. There is no one like Him, and He is good to us despite the fact that we don't deserve Him. That is grace. May His grace be with you as you try to understand how wide, how deep, and how high His love is for you. May you also come to know how far the east is from the west.

Psalm 103: 8–14

The LORD is compassionate and gracious, slow to anger, abounding in love.

He will not always accuse, nor will he harbor his anger forever; he does not treat us as our sins deserve or repay us according to our iniquities. For as high as the heavens are above the earth, so great is his love for those who fear him; as far as the east is from the west, so far has he removed our transgressions from us. As a father has compassion on his children, so the LORD has compassion on those who fear him; for he knows how we are formed, he remembers that we are dust.

From the Author

The Hope of Eliza started with the last scene where Emma is at the abortion clinic. It was written while praying to God. I felt like He gave me the plot of this book. That scene destroyed my heart. I felt Emma's pain. She was lost, confused, had been lied to, and ultimately abandoned. I felt her fear. I also saw her unborn child. I saw an innocent life that was about to be destroyed. A human that might never have the chance at life. A baby that had a destiny. God has a plan for every life. What are we missing because they no longer have their lives?

I've seen the statistics, heard the arguments, but that is not why I wrote this book. I wrote it to reach the Emmas and save the Elizas of this world. I wrote it because I care for them, hurt for them, and will fight for them.

In the fight over abortion, I have heard both sides say angry and hurtful things. I have seen each one spew facts to support their side. To me abortion has more than two sides. The topic of abortion is more personal to me because abortion deals with people. People as in plural. I am especially concerned that in our tenacity to rescue the baby; that we ignore or worse alienate the mother of the child. She, too, is often the victim. She is often abandoned if she thinks about keeping the baby. If she decides to keep the baby, she is subjected to the shame of carrying the child, sometimes the pressure causes her to drop out of school. Sometimes, she has no financial support.

In order to protect herself and her reputation she decides to have an abortion. Something that society tells her is not only okay, but is the right decision. Then who is left to pick up the pieces of her broken heart? Shari Rigby's story has touched me to the depths of my heart. See her testimony at the end of "October Baby" the movie. Hers is a story about her journey of forgiveness of herself.

My goal in writing this book is to raise the awareness of what mothers who consider having abortion go through. My hope is that readers will fall in love with Emma and have compassion on her, and will fall in love with Eliza and fight for her life. That they would become The Hope of Eliza by reaching out to the Emmas of our world.

I firmly believe that abortion should be illegal because it kills a child and breaks a mother. This subject is close to my heart, and I hope my passion transcends the words on the page that I write.

About the Author

Tawnye Dee Kanumuri was born in southern California but grew up in Colorado Springs. She is the oldest of eight children. Her father, Gary, a custom homebuilder, taught her right from wrong and how to be a patriotic American and stand up for her personal beliefs. Her mother, Ola, was a stay-at-home mom for most of her life and is responsible for shaping Tawnye into a kind and compassionate person who believes in chasing big dreams and making an impact in the world around her. Tawnye was named after her grandmother, Deloris Welty, whom everyone called Dee. Tawnye never got the privilege of meeting her grandmother but deeply misses her.

Tawnye started writing at a very early age and always dreamed of becoming an author. Her parents and husband nurtured this dream until it became a reality in 2014, when she published her first book, *The Hope of Eliza*, at age twenty-five. The stories of Emma and Eliza were birthed from Tawnye's passion for writing and for the hurting. Though fiction, *The Hope of Eliza* conveys her deep conviction to stand up for women and children without a voice. Its message has stirred Tawnye's heart, and she truly believes the book was God inspired.

Tawnye graduated from The University of Colorado in 2012 with a bachelor's degree in English and a minor in elementary education. She now teaches first grade in Monument, Colorado. She married the love of her life, Vamsi Kanumuri, in July 2011. They have two dogs: a Leonburger—you have to look it up—named Rocky and a puggle named Leah.

Her happy family lives in Colorado Springs, where she met her husband at a ballroom dance studio. They enjoy being with family and friends, dancing, and watching movies. She also enjoys being outdoors, where she hikes, swims, and boats. Tawnye is an avid reader. Colorado is her home because it is renowned for the beauty of the mountains and the genuineness of its people. Tawnye and her husband attend New Life Church and consider it a second home. She is in love with Jesus. His passion and love for her inspires her to write and to dream.